SHOOTING BLANKS

By the time the men had given up on trying to open the door the easy way, Clint was fitting the barrel and cylinder into place. All he focused on was following the familiar chain of movements while trying to do them fast enough to save his life.

A boot slammed against the door to buckle it within its frame. The door held against that first kick, buying Clint a precious fraction of a second. It didn't hold up against the second kick, however, and came slamming inward to let the men charge into Clint's room with their weapons at the ready. By the time those men spotted the table where Clint was sitting, the modified Colt was put together and pointed directly at them.

Acting on pure reflex, Clint aimed the gun as soon as he got it in his hand. He squeezed the trigger, even though one thing was nagging at the back of his mind.

The hammer reached back and snapped forward, landing squarely on an empty chamber.

The Colt was in one piece again, but that piece didn't include any ammunition . . .

THE GUNSMITH

281

RING OF FIRE

J. R. ROBERTS

JOVE BOOKS, NEW YORK

THE BERKLEY PUBLISHING GROUP
Published by the Penguin Group
Penguin Group (USA) Inc.
375 Hudson Street, New York, New York 10014, USA
Penguin Group (Canada), 10 Alcorn Avenue, Toronto, Ontario M4V 3B2, Canada
(a division of Pearson Penguin Canada Inc.)
Penguin Books Ltd., 80 Strand, London WC2R 0RL, England
Penguin Group Ireland, 25 St. Stephen's Green, Dublin 2, Ireland (a division of Penguin Books Ltd.)
Penguin Group (Australia), 250 Camberwell Road, Camberwell, Victoria 3124, Australia
(a division of Pearson Australia Group Pty. Ltd.)
Penguin Books India Pvt. Ltd., 11 Community Centre, Panchsheel Park, New Delhi—110 017, India
Penguin Group (NZ), Cnr. Airborne and Rosedale Roads, Albany, Auckland 1310, New Zealand
(a division of Pearson New Zealand Ltd.)
Penguin Books (South Africa) (Pty.) Ltd., 24 Sturdee Avenue, Rosebank, Johannesburg 2196,
South Africa

Penguin Books Ltd., Registered Offices: 80 Strand, London WC2R 0RL, England

This is a work of fiction. Names, characters, places, and incidents either are the product of the author's imagination or are used fictitiously, and any resemblance to actual persons, living or dead, business establishments, events, or locales is entirely coincidental.

RING OF FIRE

A Jove Book / published by arrangement with the author

PRINTING HISTORY
Jove edition / May 2005

ISBN: 0-515-13945-9

JOVE®
Jove Books are published by The Berkley Publishing Group,
a division of Penguin Group (USA) Inc.,
375 Hudson Street, New York, New York 10014.
JOVE is a registered trademark of Penguin Group (USA) Inc.
The "J" design is a trademark belonging to Penguin Group (USA) Inc.

PRINTED IN THE UNITED STATES OF AMERICA

10 9 8 7 6 5 4 3 2 1

ONE

The doors to the Second Chance Saloon flew open and were nearly knocked off their hinges as something heavy was tossed out onto the street. That heavy something went by the name of Wilbur Johanssen, and when his backside hit the dirt he was in no hurry to get back up again.

Wilbur sat right where he landed and took a few moments to pull a few breaths into his lungs. His ears were still ringing from the ruckus going on inside the saloon. The ringing was so loud, in fact, that he almost didn't hear the scratchy voice directed at him from the saloon's doorway.

A burly man with more than a few empty spaces in his grin glared out at Wilbur and stabbed a thick finger toward him. "And don't try showin' yer dirty face in here again!" he shouted. "If I see you in here, I won't be so gentle in tossin' yer ass out!"

Wilbur had to smirk at that. The notion that the big man in the doorway could possibly be gentle struck him as funny at that particular moment.

"I'll be sure to remember that," Wilbur said.

But the doorway was empty and the big man had already gone to look for someone else to push around within the saloon.

Wilbur flopped over and sat up, but didn't bother moving from there. It seemed appropriate for him to be sitting in the dirt just then. Anything else would have felt like too much to hope for.

Shaking his head, Wilbur patted his pockets one at a time. He wasn't surprised to find them all empty, but that didn't keep him from checking them one more time just to be sure. The last flicker of hope he felt when checking his left boot was snuffed out when he realized that the holdout spot was also empty.

"Daisy is gonna kill me," Wilbur grumbled.

The truth of the matter was that he didn't even remember reaching for those last couple of dollars secreted in his boot. That money was supposed to be off limits for dire situations. Then again, the run of cards he'd seen at the game he'd been thrown out of did strike him as something awfully close to a dire situation.

"Hello, Wilbur."

Those words drifted through the air as a subtle way to remind the man on the ground that, no matter how bad things were, they could always be worse.

Wilbur didn't have to look up to know who was speaking to him. "Evening, Danny."

Standing at well over six feet in height, Daniel O'Shea was uglier than something that had been shot, dragged into town and then run over by a team of mules. His skin was pockmarked and both front teeth were chipped in half at odd angles.

The hand that reached down to grab hold of Wilbur by the back of his shirt was calloused, thick and meaty. The owner of that hand picked Wilbur up like he was nothing and held him like a puppy that was being scolded.

"Only my friends or me mother calls me Danny," the big, ugly fellow grunted. "And you ain't neither one of those."

Wilbur tried to swallow what little moisture he had in

his mouth, but was unable to do so because he was dangling from his own collar. After a few scrambling attempts, he was finally able to get his feet beneath him so he could support his own weight.

"Funny to see you here," Wilbur said, tugging at his collar without trying to make it look as if he was attempting to escape the big man's grasp. "I was just going to talk to your employer tomorrow morning."

"Save the bullshit," Danny said, while shaking Wilbur with every syllable. "And don't try to talk your way out of this."

Letting out a defeated breath, Wilbur let himself dangle from his collar. The light-headedness that came from the lack of air was something of a relief. "I know," he said. "Too late for that."

Danny looked confused, disappointed and then angered that his next words had been taken from right out of his mouth. "Well . . . it . . . it is too late!" Focusing in on the man dangling from the end of his fist, Danny's eyes narrowed and filled with nothing but anger. "You borrowed some money from Mr. Gilliam and he wants it back."

"But, it's not due until next week!"

"I suppose you've got some of it for me, then?"

"No, I . . ."

When the sentence trailed out of Wilbur's mouth without being finished, it hung in the air like a cloud.

Danny smirked and nodded as though he'd finally gotten the punch line of a joke. "Yeah. That's just what Mr. Gilliam said you'd say." Still holding on to Wilbur by the shirt collar, Danny brought him close enough so every bit of spit that flew from his mouth landed on Wilbur's face. "This is the first and last warning you get. Understand?"

Wincing as much from the spittle flying from Danny's mouth as from the reek of the bigger man's breath, Wilbur nodded.

"Good. Now how much you got right now?" Danny asked.

"Nothing," Wilbur replied without so much as a moment's hesitation. "I've got nothing left. I lost it all."

Danny bared his teeth and lifted Wilbur up higher so he could swat at the smaller man's pockets with his free hand. "You got to have something."

When he was done going through Wilbur's pockets, Danny tossed him aside as if he was a piece of rotten fish. "What about that on yer finger?"

Wilbur held his hands up so he could look at them himself, but couldn't figure out what Danny was talking about.

"Yer ring," Danny grunted. "Hand it over."

The gold band around Wilbur's finger had been there so long that it was as much a part of him as his fingers themselves. Actually, it was more vital to him than his fingers, because he would have handed over any of them more willingly than he would part with that ring.

"It's my wedding ring," Wilbur said. "You can't—"

"I said hand it over!"

"But my wife gave this to me. She worked herself to—"

"Give it to me, or I'll take her instead."

Those words stopped Wilbur like a sharp smack in the face. As much as he wanted to make Danny regret making that threat, he knew that there wasn't a way for him to do such a thing. He didn't carry a gun, and even if he did he doubted that he would consider drawing it against a reputed killer like Daniel O'Shea.

Even so, Wilbur's hand balled into a fist. Before he knew what he was doing, his arm was drawing back and snapping out again to send that fist straight up into Danny's jaw.

Unfortunately, Wilbur's fist made it less than halfway to its destination before smacking against Danny's calloused palm.

Danny's lips curled into a smile as his fingers curled around the punch he'd caught out of thin air.

"You got sand," Danny said before sending his free hand straight into Wilbur's temple. "No brains, but a bit of sand."

The impact rattled Wilbur's entire world.

One moment, he was making a desperate ploy to save his last remaining bit of pride, and the next moment, he was toppling backward into a pool of black with a throbbing pain settling into the middle of his skull.

Wilbur didn't feel his back hit the dirt.

He didn't hear Danny laughing at him.

He didn't even notice the people stepping over and around him as they came and went from the Second Chance Saloon.

TWO

The first thing Wilbur saw when he opened his eyes was the sign painted over the saloon's front door that read, SECOND CHANCE. His eyes focused on those two words like they were all that remained in his world. The funny part of it all was that he knew he'd run clean out of chances and wasn't about to get another one anytime soon.

"You all right down there?"

The question came from above and behind the spot where Wilbur was laying. Even though he'd heard the words, Wilbur didn't see much sense in responding to them. He seemed to belong right where he was: in the dirt.

Enough sunlight was breaking through the clouds for Wilbur to see the shadow of a man who came walking up behind him. The long shadow covered him and stayed put as the man who'd spoken to him moments ago came to a stop.

"You don't look too good, mister," came the voice once again. "How long have you been sitting there?"

"Just leave me alone," Wilbur grumbled as he shifted around and took a halfhearted swing at whoever was standing behind him. Although Wilbur's fist didn't make contact with anything, it did cause the man behind him to take a quick half step back.

6

At first, Wilbur thought the other person was leaving. But the same shadow merely moved around him as the one casting it stepped over to look at his face. The first thing Wilbur saw was a pair of battered boots. As he looked up, his eyes moved along a set of well-worn jeans, and then stopped once he saw the holster strapped around the man's waist.

"Oh, Jesus," Wilbur groaned. "I guess you're out to kill me. Might as well! I won't try to stop you."

The man looked down at Wilbur with a fair mix of confusion and amusement. Although he didn't find the other man outright funny, he was carrying on without being noticed by anyone else around him. All the other people walking down the street didn't so much as look at Wilbur. Instead, they just kept on doing whatever they were doing and stepping over the man when they had to.

Kneeling down so he was able to get a better look at Wilbur's face, the man extended a hand while putting on a comforting smile. "I'm not going to hurt you, mister," he said. "I just thought you might want to get out of the street before you get trampled."

Wilbur's eyes fixed on the man before he accepted the hand being offered to him. "You mean, you're not one of Mr. O'Shea's men?"

"Nope," the man replied while closing his hand around Wilbur's and lifting him up to his feet. "My name's Clint Adams. I just got into town a day ago."

As soon as Wilbur was on his own two feet he felt the throbbing in his head return and his knees start to buckle. Luckily, Clint hadn't let go of him all the way and was able to steady him before he toppled over again.

"You look like hell," Clint said. "Did you get robbed?"

"No, it was . . ." Stopping himself in midsentence, Wilbur pulled his hand back so he could get a look at it. His ring finger was scraped, bruised and swollen to almost double its size. It was also missing the gold band that had previously been around it.

"Aw shit," Wilbur grumbled.

Clint took a look at what the other man was staring at and nodded grimly. "Someone stole your ring?"

"Yeah. Dammit!"

"Looks like they had to fight for it. It could have been worse."

"Really? And how do you figure that?"

"They could have cut your finger off rather than rip the ring off you like that. Judging by the state of that finger, I'd say whoever took your ring was plenty strong enough to save themselves some trouble and take your finger."

"Strong enough, maybe. But not nearly smart enough."

"Well, either way, it looks to me like things could have been a whole lot worse."

"Not from where I'm sitting."

Clint had been walking down the street when he'd noticed Wilbur lying there. Thanks to the way the locals stepped easily around Wilbur, Clint was surprised that he'd spotted the man at all. Now that he had, he was beginning to see why everyone else was more inclined to just let him sit wherever he was.

"Look," Clint said. "I was on my way to get something to eat. You hungry?"

"I don't need your charity."

"I wasn't offering any charity. I just asked if you wanted something to eat."

Wilbur looked at Clint and studied him for a moment. He could see no hint of meanness in Clint's eyes. In fact, Clint's face was the friendliest he'd seen in quite a while. Of course, considering the company he'd been keeping, that wasn't saying too much. Still, Wilbur knew a bit of genuine goodwill when it came his way.

"Sure," Wilbur said. "I could use a bite to eat."

Clint nodded and started walking to the restaurant that he'd been heading for when he'd first spotted the man in the street. "I don't think I caught your name."

"It's Wilbur. Wilbur Johanssen."

"Well, Wilbur, I suppose you'll be wanting to stop by the marshal's office to report what happened."

"No reason."

"We'll just see about that," Clint said. "I mean, considering where I found you, there's got to be some hope that things will turn around."

Wilbur glanced up to where Clint was pointing.

As before, the sign over the saloon's door was still there.

"Second chance, huh?" Wilbur groaned. "I'd say I'm on my fifth or sixth chance at least."

"Just so long as you get another one, right?"

Noticing the genuine optimism in Clint's voice, Wilbur chuckled to spite himself. "Yeah. I guess so." He flexed his hand before rubbing the scraped and bruised finger that had been circled by a ring of gold a matter of hours ago. "I guess things could be worse."

THREE

Los Tejanos was a town that seemed as though it had been in its spot since the first winds blew across New Mexico. Its streets were crooked and lined with some buildings that were so old their walls appeared to have been petrified in place.

Like other stubborn towns, Los Tejanos refused to crumble no matter how much hard luck befell it. Railroad bids came and went, but never quite landed. Gold and silver mines sprouted up nearby, but never really panned out. Even a few stagecoach companies started to build a station there, but always found some better spot in a neighboring town.

All of that considered, Los Tejanos was still there.

Like the town itself, the people who lived there were tough as nails and didn't put up with any guff. They had eyes that were all but shut against the blazing sun and skin that hardly even felt the heat of the nearby desert. They didn't suffer fools lightly.

That's why Clint found it easier to believe why they'd stepped around Wilbur Johanssen rather than help him up.

"I don't know what I'm going to do," Wilbur sighed. He'd been whining ever since they'd walked into the restaurant. In fact, he had yet to pull his sorry face up out of the bowl of oatmeal which was the only thing he'd ordered.

Clint watched the man poke at his cooling bowl of oats, wondering if he was actually going to see a grown man cry. Wilbur looked to be in his late thirties, although Clint's first guess at the man's age would have tacked on an additional ten to fifteen years.

Wilbur had a light complexion that had been turned nearly beet red by the New Mexico sun. His light brown hair was cut short at odd angles, with several chunks much shorter than others. It was that sort of hair which normally marked a single man, since that was the sort of job done by a man on himself using nothing more than a knife or razor.

Following Clint's eyes, Wilbur reached up and patted his hand on top of his own head. Instantly finding several uneven patches, Wilbur shrugged and said, "I cut it myself, but I tell my wife that I go to the barber once every other week or so. That way, I can bring home ten times the amount of money I'd use to get a haircut when I win at cards."

"And does that happen very often?" Clint asked.

The light that had flared up in Wilbur's eyes dwindled straightaway. "Not as such, no."

Clint shook his head at Wilbur as though he was looking at a misbehaving child. He hadn't meant to treat the other man as such, but he couldn't exactly help himself; especially with Wilbur hunched over his bowl of oatmeal.

"Gambling isn't the best thing to do if you can't afford it," Clint said. "You've got to know that much."

"Yeah, I do."

Seeing the scraped finger wrapped around Wilbur's spoon, Clint asked, "You weren't just robbed, were you?"

"No. Not as such."

"How much do you owe?"

Wilbur rolled his eyes and pushed his spoon through his

oatmeal, which made him look even more like a grumbling kid. After scooping up some oatmeal, he stuck the spoon in his mouth and shrugged again. "Not much, really. They took my wedding ring, so that should keep them happy for a while."

Clint laughed and shook his head while cutting into the steak he'd ordered to go along with his batch of scrambled eggs. "Then you must have borrowed it from some pretty impatient people if they were willing to yank your wedding ring from your finger and leave you knocked out in the street like that. Most folks wouldn't go through so much trouble to recover not too much money."

"Yeah, you're right."

"How much did you borrow?" Clint asked before taking a bite of his steak.

"Fifteen hundred dollars," Wilbur said. "More or less."

Clint froze with his teeth halfway into his steak. He was still holding his fork up to his mouth when he asked, "Fifteen hundred? Did I hear you right?"

Wilbur nodded.

"And how fancy was your wedding ring?"

"Just a gold band, but it was all we could afford. My wife even insisted on paying for it herself."

"That's admirable, Wilbur, but wasn't exactly my point. Do you think it looked to be worth anything close to fifteen hundred dollars?"

Wilbur cast his eyes downward again and shook his head.

For a moment, Clint felt bad for the guy. Then again, he'd seen what happened to men who got a little too full of themselves at the poker table. "Do you think they'll be back for the rest?" he asked.

"I reckon so," Wilbur replied with a shrug. "But I'll have it for them. I wouldn't be so foolish as to put off paying someone like Mr. Gilliam."

Clint lowered his fork and allowed himself to chew his steak. After everything he'd heard, finding Wilbur in the street that way didn't really seem like such a surprise anymore. The real surprise was that Wilbur was alive at all.

"You're a lucky man, Wilbur. There's plenty of men out there who'd kill you for holding out that much money. Either that, or they would have hurt you a whole lot worse."

Now, it was Wilbur's turn to laugh. "Lucky? That's the first time I've ever heard anyone call me that."

"At least you're still breathing," Clint said. "And you've got a hot meal. I find things seem a whole lot better on a full stomach."

With that, Wilbur dropped his spoon into the remains of his oatmeal and pushed the bowl away from him. "Actually, I can't eat another bite. Sorry I can't pay for my part of the bill, but—"

"Don't worry about it," Clint interrupted. "It's my treat."

Suddenly, Wilbur's eyes snapped back and forth between his bowl of cold, half-eaten oatmeal and Clint's steak. The regret was plain enough to see, as was the disgusted way he let out his breath.

Clint didn't have to be a mind reader to know what was going through Wilbur's mind at that moment. Smirking subtly, he said, "You can order a steak if you want."

For a moment, Wilbur perked up a bit. That was short-lived, however, as he slumped right back into his seat again. "Nah, but thanks anyway. I'd just feel like I'd owe someone else and I already owe too much to too many folks already."

"Suit yourself." Clint took a bite of his eggs and then a sip from his coffee. All the while, he kept a close eye on Wilbur. "You live around here?"

"Yeah. I should probably be getting home. My wife'll be worried."

"Take care of yourself, Wilbur."

But he'd already pushed away from the table and started heading for the door.

Something else had caught Clint's eye as well, but he didn't bring it up to Wilbur. The guy seemed to have enough on his plate already without having to worry about being watched by a couple of men who looked like they ate broken glass for breakfast.

FOUR

Clint finished up his breakfast as quickly as he could. The men watching Wilbur leave the restaurant weren't in any particular hurry, which meant that Clint was able to enjoy what remained of his meal before leaving too much on his plate.

After Wilbur had left, the other two hung back for a while and then walked out after him. Clint was on their trail a few moments later, making a sort of train with him at the end and Wilbur leading the way.

If there was any doubt that the other two men were following Wilbur, those doubts were erased when they latched on to the poor fellow and dogged his trail. One of those men was built like a pile of bricks wrapped up in worn, leathery skin. A beard covered his face, but looked more like a patch of fur that had been hastily stuck on to his chin.

The second man was a bit smaller, but not by much. He wore a thick mustache over a sneering expression that seemed to be a permanent fixture upon his face. Of the two, he seemed to be more of a follower since he kept looking to the first man for instructions.

Even from the distance he'd put between himself and the others, Clint could see that both of the men following

15

Wilbur were heeled. They wore their guns strapped low around their waists and tied off just above their knees. Most men who wore their guns like that were more concerned about looking bad than actually being quick draws.

There were exceptions to every rule, but the two men dogging Wilbur's trail scowled at everyone who dared to look in their direction. They strutted like roosters in a henhouse, which made Clint figure his first impression of the pair had been right on the money.

They were full of hot air.

They were also plenty confident in their ability to take Wilbur down at any moment and were just waiting for the proper time to present itself. The most likely reason for that was because they probably had already done so at least once already.

Clint would have bet good money that these were the same men who'd left Wilbur in the street with a scraped finger, a knock on the head and no wedding ring. And just when he was thinking that Wilbur could deal with his own problems, Clint saw the bigger of those two men pick up his pace while reaching down toward his gun.

"Where do you think he's goin'?"

The man who'd asked that question was the smaller of the two following Wilbur Johanssen. His lip was covered with a brushy mustache, which just so happened to be one of the man's finer points. The rest of him looked as though he'd been chewed up and spit out. He was called Braber, and his most redeeming physical quality was that he didn't look as bad as the man directly beside him.

O'Shea shrugged and spat a wad of tobacco juice onto the ground. "Probably goin' home to hide. That's what I'd do if I was him."

The second man smirked lewdly. "Yeah. 'Specially if my wife looked like his."

"Yeah. I heard that."

"Should we follow him home?" Braber asked.

"You think he's got any money there?"

"Probably not. We just checked there not too long ago."

"Then let's see if he got any from that fella he had breakfast with."

"You think he'll hand it over?"

In response to that, O'Shea reached for the gun strapped to his side. "I don't give a shit what he hands over. We're takin' everything he's got. I'm sick of wasting time on this asshole."

Braber smiled wide enough to split his face in two. Before he could reach for his own pistol, he felt a rush of air and something else graze past his arm.

The rush of air was so quick and so subtle that Braber didn't really pay too much attention to it. Just then, his eyes found what had caused the gust and then went wide as saucers. He hadn't seen the arm reaching past him until it was too late. By that time, it was too late for O'Shea as well.

Clint reached past the second man and plucked the first one's pistol from its holster before anyone made a move against him. In fact, the two burly men were so focused on Wilbur that they seemed to have been planted in molasses while Clint was streaking right through them.

O'Shea's gun left its holster with only the sound of iron against leather to mark the occasion. Clint knew he'd been spotted by the other man and was already moving to do something about it before a single sound could leave Braber's mouth.

Still reaching past Braber, Clint tightened his grip around the gun he'd taken and drove his elbow straight back into Braber's chest. There was some power in the blow, but only enough to put Braber off balance without doing any real harm. In fact, Clint took note of the way his elbow bounced against the other man's solid chest.

When O'Shea's hand found nothing but empty space

where his gun should have been, he wheeled around to get a look at what was going on behind him. His eyes were narrowed angrily, but his words caught in his throat when he saw that someone besides Braber was standing directly behind him.

Holding O'Shea's gun in one hand, Clint tossed it across to his other hand with a quick flick of his wrist. Before he even caught that gun, he'd already drawn his modified Colt.

"Well now," Clint said as he pointed one gun at each of the other two men. "We seem to have an interesting situation here."

FIVE

Even though they were looking at Clint, neither O'Shea or Braber could believe what they were seeing. They both took turns gaping at him, and then at each other before one of them finally collected themselves enough to speak.

"What the hell do you think you're doing?" O'Shea asked.

"I was just going to ask you two the same thing."

Braber licked his lips anxiously as his fingers curled and uncurled over the grip of his pistol.

Seeing that, O'Shea snarled, "What the hell are you waiting for? Shoot this son of a bitch already!"

Clint fixed his eyes on to Braber while making sure to keep O'Shea in the corner of his field of vision. Cocking his head slightly, Clint put on a smirk and said, "I'm not certain he wants to do that."

Between the tone in Clint's voice, the certainty in his eyes and the gun in his hand, Braber was inclined to agree with that statement. Of course, he wasn't about to say that much out loud.

But Braber didn't have to say a word for O'Shea to know his partner wasn't about to move anytime soon.

Glancing back to Clint, he asked, "So you got our attention. Now what?"

Clint looked quickly down the street and saw that Wilbur had continued along his way. That meant he was either smart enough to know when to leave, or completely oblivious of what was happening around him. Whichever it was, Clint was just glad that Wilbur was gone.

"Why would you want to spend a perfectly good day following around someone like that?" Clint asked.

O'Shea laughed under his breath. "He owes us money. That's all you need to know."

"How much does he owe?"

"Closing in on two thousand. Who the hell are you? His mother?"

That brought a laugh to Braber's throat as well, which stuck in place the moment he got another warning glare from Clint.

"What about what you stole from him earlier?" Clint asked. "Did you count that toward what he owes you or was that just a bonus for yourself?"

Leaning in with an openmouthed sneer, O'Shea said, "That was interest. Hell, that ring of his was prolly made'a tin anyhow."

Since he hadn't mentioned what had been stolen exactly, Clint now knew for certain that these were the men who'd jumped Wilbur and left him lying in the street. He could also tell that these men had some definite plans for Wilbur and that not one of them were good.

"Kind of hard for a dead man to pay up, isn't it?" Clint asked.

"I still don't see what business this is of yers," O'Shea snarled. "So you should either drop them guns or put 'em to work."

The moments that followed that ultimatum passed by on turtles' legs. Other folks were walking by not too far away, but none of them were aware of the standoff happening so close to them.

Even though he didn't make a move, it was plain to see that Braber wanted to be anywhere but where he was standing. The fact that he didn't move was more a testament to his fear than his resolve.

Finally, Clint lowered the guns. He dropped the Colt back into its holster and tossed the gun he'd taken from O'Shea well away from both of the other two men.

"There," Clint said. "Now we can talk reasonably."

"Fuck reasonable," O'Shea snorted as he started walking toward his gun.

In a flash, Clint's hand was around the grip of his Colt and the pistol was halfway out of its holster. "No need for that just yet," Clint warned.

Braber had his own gun on him, but still didn't look confident enough to draw it. O'Shea regarded him as he might regard something wet and smelly on the bottom of his boot.

"How much does Wilbur owe you?" Clint asked.

To that, O'Shea merely smiled. "He don't owe me a cent. He owes Mr. Gilliam plenty, though."

"Mr. Gilliam?"

"That's right. You ever heard of him?"

"No," Clint replied. "Is there a reason why I should have?"

"Only because he's the type of man to eat assholes like you for supper."

"All that, and we haven't even met. Usually it takes folks a bit more than that before they want to kill me."

Up until now, O'Shea had looked either confused or pissed off. Now, however, his mood shifted to more of an amused tolerance. "You got sand, mister. I'll give you that much. What's yer name?"

Clint had been around far too long to just give out that

information. He wasn't exactly full of himself, but he knew only too well what effect his reputation would have on men like these other two. The situation was already tense enough. There was no need to add any fuel to the fire.

"I'm just the type of man who doesn't like to watch an unarmed man get shot down," Clint replied. "Let's leave it at that."

O'Shea shook his head. "You cross me, you're crossing Mr. Gilliam as well. And when you do that, he'll find out who you are, who your family is, where they're staying and everything else under the sun."

"Then we'd best just part ways right now," Clint said in an even tone. "So get your pistol, walk away and cool off."

O'Shea stepped over to where his gun had landed and stood there for a moment before reaching for it. He eyed Clint suspiciously as if he expected him to draw the Colt at any time.

Holding his hands out to show his good intentions, Clint stepped away from both men and circled around until he was standing between them and the direction Wilbur had headed. Once O'Shea had holstered his gun, Clint held his ground as both men walked straight toward him.

Shaking his head, Clint said, "Pick another direction."

"Why? You got something against a man collecting what's owed to him?"

"You took everything he had. That should keep you satisfied for a little while."

Surprisingly enough, it was Braber who started to walk forward when he heard that. Of course, he was probably expecting O'Shea to stop him.

"Fine," O'Shea said, while thrusting his hand out to block Braber's path. "We know where Johanssen lives. We can find him. Just like we can find you."

The threat of what would happen after that wasn't too far beneath the surface of O'Shea's words. Clint picked up on it without a problem, but didn't allow his face to shift one bit in response to it.

Judging by O'Shea's expression, however, one might have thought that he'd just delivered a knockout punch. The burly man snickered under his breath and backed away from Clint without once breaking eye contact.

"Come on, Braber," O'Shea said. "Let's get us a drink before we finish up our business."

Now was the time for Braber to act tough, which he did only after he was a bit farther away from Clint.

Watching the two strut away, Clint hoped that Wilbur didn't have any plans for the night. He'd bought the other man a night's rest, but Clint doubted he'd given him peace that would last longer than that. Still, he'd stuck his nose in far enough and saw no reason to pry any further.

Then again, other people's problems had a nasty habit of finding Clint just fine on their own.

SIX

Wilbur Johanssen lived in a humble shack near the middle of town. It was a decent enough place to live, just so long as a person didn't mind hearing the rest of the town's business almost every hour of every day. He'd built the place with his own two hands back when Los Tejanos had been just a few shops established by a few rich Texans.

The town had grown since then, and the noisiest parts of that growth always seemed to happen right outside of Wilbur's doorstep. What had once been a scenic view was now blocked by a general store. Most of his friendly neighbors had all moved on to be replaced by lost, drunken cowboys.

All of that bothered him a little less, however, when the door was opened before he could lay a hand on it and he was greeted by a warm, comforting smile.

"Wilbur! I'm so glad you're home!" exclaimed a woman in her late twenties wearing a simple checked dress that hugged a finely curved body.

Going by the look on her face, she was the princess in a castle and Wilbur was her returning prince. She smiled like an angel and rushed forward with open arms waiting to be wrapped around him.

Wilbur couldn't help but smile as well. The woman always smelled like fresh air and home cooking. Her long, wavy brown hair brushed against his face like a fragrant mist as her soft, supple body pressed tightly against him.

"Where have you been?" she asked after squeezing him tightly. Holding him at arm's length, she looked at him with growing concern. "I woke up and couldn't find you anywhere. I was just about to go look for you myself."

"I'm right here, Daisy," Wilbur said in the most comforting voice he could manage. "No need to fuss."

It was obvious that Daisy had some other words for him, but she kept from saying them out loud. Instead, she took in a deep breath and nodded. "You're right. But will you at least tell me what happened? I fixed breakfast for you. It's getting cold, but that's what you should expect when you stay out until the break of dawn."

Allowing himself to be pulled into the house, Wilbur nodded and said, "I know. I deserve plenty of bad things, but instead I got the best of the lot."

"What do you mean?"

Wilbur wrapped his arms around her and kicked the door shut before planting a kiss on her that took the young woman's breath away. "I got you," he said. "And I thank the Lord for that each and every day."

Daisy smiled broadly and melted into his arms. Her hands traced over his shoulders and down along his arms in a path that was all too familiar to her husband.

Wilbur felt his heart skip a beat. Whenever she was feeling especially close to him, Daisy always liked to run her fingers over his wedding band and then thread her fingers through his. At that moment, with things feeling better than they had for a while, Wilbur did not want to ruin them by going into the story of where his wedding band had gone.

As soon as he felt her hand run over his shoulder, Wilbur reached around to grasp her by the waist and pull her close. Daisy's eyes went wide with excitement and she pulled in a quick, little breath.

"My word, something has come over you," she said breathlessly.

"I'm just happy to be home."

And just when he thought he'd made it through the potentially rough waters, Wilbur noticed how his wife was examining his face. The excitement that had been in her eyes only moments ago had been replaced by fear and she pulled away from him so she could examine a little more of him.

"Oh, my God," she said. "What happened to you?"

After everything else that had gone on that night, Wilbur had forgotten about the knock to the head which had left him lying in the street. Oddly enough, that seemed rather small in comparison to the other messes that enveloped his life.

"It's nothing," he said, twisting away from her so he didn't have to be under such close scrutiny. "Just got into a fight."

"A fight? What happened?" But even before Wilbur got a chance to respond, Daisy was placing her hands upon her hips and narrowing her eyes. "You were at the saloon again, weren't you?"

Wilbur tried to come up with something he could say that wouldn't make matters worse. It wasn't that he wanted to hide anything from his wife. He just figured that there would be plenty of time to make her worry later. At least he'd figured on resting up a bit before pulling the smile off her face.

The expression Wilbur had on as he thought those things was more than enough to answer Daisy's question. "You were gambling," she stated firmly. "How much did you lose?"

"I didn't—"

"How much, Wilbur?"

"I broke even. Maybe lost a dollar or two."

Daisy let out a breath which seemed to soften her entire demeanor. Gently, she reached out to touch the dark bruise on his temple. "Then this is about the money you still owe?"

"Yeah," he replied, wincing as her fingers grazed the sensitive wound. "That's what it was about."

"And is that why you were so late?"

"I got knocked out in front of the saloon and left there. I just woke up a little while ago. Some stranger bought me some coffee and I came right home." Lowering his head, he added sheepishly, "I didn't want to worry you, Daisy. That's all."

Pulling him toward the bed at the other end of the room, Daisy went over to a washbasin, soaked a rag and then wrung it out. Shaking her head, she dabbed the wet cloth against Wilbur's temple and cleaned off the rest of his face.

"You can never disappoint me," she said. "I know that's what you're thinking. I can see it in your eyes."

"You always know more about what's going on than I do."

"That's why you married me," she said with a smirk. "Someone needs to keep their wits in this family. I also know what will make you feel better."

After pushing him back onto the bed, Daisy climbed on top of him and slowly began to unbutton the front of her dress. At that moment, despite everything else in his life, Wilbur Johanssen felt like the luckiest man alive.

SEVEN

Most people who met Wilbur Johanssen usually thought that if he had any luck at all, it was bad. All they needed to do was watch the way he played cards, earned his money or even crossed the street to arrive at that conclusion. In fact, Wilbur was usually one of the first to admit to that very thing.

That opinion changed, however, when that same person got a look at Mrs. Johanssen.

Normally, most folks thought that Daisy had to be a relative or in-law of Wilbur's for her to share his last name. Once she smiled, held his hand and said she was Wilbur's wife, anyone who thought that Wilbur's luck was entirely bad knew they were mistaken.

Most men imagined touching Daisy's soft skin or feeling her lips upon theirs, but didn't get much further than that. She never gave anyone but her husband the faintest glimmer of hope in that direction. And when she did give her attention to him, she gave it without question and without holding back.

They'd been married for years and they still acted like newlyweds. This night was no exception.

Arching her back, Daisy peeled the dress down over herself until it was gathered up around her waist. Full, rounded breasts were accentuated by the rays of sunlight drifting through the room. The golden light made her naturally tanned skin seem almost like bronze, while also illuminating the streaks of blonde in her hair.

Daisy's small, dark nipples were erect even before Wilbur's hands found them. When he did start to massage her, Daisy let out a contented sigh while closing her eyes and leaning back just a bit.

Wilbur looked up at her, watching every little move she made and listening to every little sound. Even now, he wondered if she was going to ever wise up and leave him someday. But before those doubts could set themselves in too deeply, he felt her start to undress him.

"How's this?" she asked in a whisper. "Feeling better?"

Leaning back to allow her to unbutton his shirt and take it off of him, Wilbur nodded. "Oh yes. Much better."

"Good." Shifting on top of him, she took her dress all the way off and kicked it onto the floor. "How about now?" she asked, leaning her head down so her hair spilled over her shoulders and onto her breasts like a silken curtain.

"Even better."

After years of marriage, they didn't have to speak or give any other hints when they were being intimate. Their bodies shifted in perfect harmony as Daisy lifted herself up a bit so Wilbur could get undressed the rest of the way.

When Wilbur's head hit his pillow, he was looking up at her wearing nothing but an eager smile. She returned the smile without question while reaching between her legs to fit him inside of her.

Daisy's hands closed around his erect penis, guiding it to the warm patch of hair between her legs. She eased herself down, taking him in, while letting out a slow, easy breath.

As Wilbur reached up to touch her, he almost felt as though he was doing something forbidden. It almost seemed odd that a woman as beautiful as Daisy wanted him to put his hands upon her. But when he touched her naked skin, Wilbur heard a contented sigh from his wife as she began to rock back and forth on top of him in earnest.

Outside their modest home, the rest of the town was going about its life. Sounds and voices drifted in through the flimsy walls of the Johanssen residence. Inside the place, however, Wilbur felt like he was in a sanctuary. His money troubles were the furthest thing from his mind and his naked angel was making him feel better than he had any right to feel.

Daisy opened her eyes and looked down at him. Her hair was tousled and her face reflected the pleasure that was going through her at that moment. When he pumped his hips up at just the right moment, she let out a happy squeal and looked down at him with renewed excitement.

"You always know just what to do," she moaned. From there, Daisy placed her hands on his chest and ground her hips in little circles while riding him. She knew exactly what to do as well.

Even as his flesh was tingling with the touch of his wife's caresses, Wilbur couldn't keep from wondering how long his happiness might last. He wasn't even thinking about the happiness she was giving him at that moment, but in general.

Daisy was too good for him.

That thought came into Wilbur's mind now; just as it did most every other time. Just looking at her trim, naked body on top of him and the perfect way her breasts swayed as she rode him was enough to make Wilbur think he'd already died and gone to Heaven.

His hands moved over her, running along her sides and coming to rest upon her hips. He could feel her muscles tensing as she took his cock slowly in and out of her. When she looked down at him, Daisy smiled and placed her hands on top of his.

"Come on," she whispered while rolling onto her side and taking him right along with her. "You know what I want."

Daisy laid on her back and placed her hands on Wilbur's shoulders as he settled on top of her. She watched him expectantly as her breaths came in a series of quickening pants.

The luckiest man in the world.

That phrase drifted through Wilbur's head as he felt his body rub against Daisy's smooth skin. That phrase echoed even louder through him when he took a moment to let his eyes wander over her naked, waiting body.

Daisy's stomach rose and fell as if she'd been running, but most of that was purely her own anxiousness for him to get back inside of her. The lips of her vagina were wet and waiting for him as well, and when he glanced down there, she spread her legs open just a bit wider.

From there, Wilbur's instincts took over and he positioned himself between her thighs so he could slip inside of her. She wrapped around him in a hot, wet embrace. When he buried himself in all the way, they both let out a sigh that had been building up over the last couple of seconds.

"There, now," Daisy whispered. "I can tell you're feeling better."

"I am," Wilbur said as he started pumping in and out of her. "I feel like the luckiest man alive."

Daisy closed her eyes and gripped his shoulders even tighter as he pounded into her with building force. She started to say something, but her breath was taken away before she could get out a single word. Finally, speaking in a partial moan, she said, "We're both lucky. Don't ever forget that."

Wilbur's hands moved up and down along his wife's body. One moment, he was feeling the sides of her breasts, and in the next he was kneading the flesh of her backside. All of it was perfection and at that moment, he had no doubt that he deserved every bit of her.

It seemed that Daisy could feel this change within him as well, since she relaxed and wrapped her arms and legs around him. She was groaning louder with every thrust until she'd finally handed herself over to her own pleasure and let out a trembling, shuddering breath.

Every time Wilbur pumped into her, he felt like he was taking one more step closer to the edge of a cliff. Judging by the way Daisy was digging her fingernails into his shoulders and straining with every muscle, she was approaching the edge of that very same cliff.

They toppled over the edge within moments of each other. Both of them were so overpowered by their climax that they couldn't speak, breathe or make any noise whatsoever.

Wilbur opened his eyes and found Daisy looking up at him like he was a king.

"Yep," he thought. "The luckiest man in the world."

EIGHT

Clint had heard plenty of things about the town of Los Tejanos. They ranged anywhere from rumors of outlaws that passed through there all the way to local legends regarding fortunes made and lost in the saloons. Being at the center of more rumors than he cared to think about himself, Clint was inclined to believe very little of the ones he heard now.

Still, that didn't mean that he discounted every last thing he'd heard about Los Tejanos. Although there was plenty being said that he couldn't believe, Clint tended to take a few of the rumors at face value. That was mainly due to the fact that one of the town's founding fathers was a personal friend of his.

Mark Bradshaw was a rich old piece of work who talked, walked and breathed everything that characterized a Texan. He was a big man with an even bigger mouth and he didn't mind backing up everything that came out of it.

Bradshaw had a nose for money and was always looking for ways to make more. For him, founding his own town was an investment. Pure and simple. He looked at it as a venture of capital, just as he'd looked at helping out with a bit of the funding for Rick's Place down in West Texas.

Rick Hartman was one of Clint's oldest friends and a fine businessman in his own right. But every businessman needed the occasional investor, which was how he'd come into the acquaintance of Mark Bradshaw.

It wasn't anything complicated. Just a simple investment when Rick had needed some help and things had already worked out just fine for both parties. Throughout the course of that investment, Clint had been introduced to Bradshaw and the two had swapped stories over a long night of beers and poker.

Even though Clint had only met him once, Mark Bradshaw wasn't exactly the type of man someone forgot. All it took was the mention of the Texan's name and Clint was immediately reminded of the big man with the waxed mustache that curled up at the ends like a set of silver hooks.

Clint hadn't really expected to hear much from Bradshaw since the two men didn't exactly travel in the same circles most of the time. That's why, when he got the letter forwarded from Rick Hartman, Clint was more than a little surprised.

It was an invitation that was just as simple as the man who'd written it. But, also like that same man, there was always more going on than what met the eye. Clint was certain there was more going on than another poker tournament, but he decided to check it out anyhow. If he didn't, he knew that Rick would never hear the end of it. Even Bradshaw's good-natured jibes could be daunting when strung one after the other.

But more than any of that, Clint was curious to see just what the Texan had up his sleeve this time. Besides, it had been a while since he'd been in that portion of New Mexico.

All of that brought Clint into where he was standing at that moment.

Clint had been in a few fancy offices before, but none quite like the one belonging to Mark Bradshaw. This office somehow managed to look bigger on the inside than the storefront and building enclosing it did on the outside.

Every inch of the room was a tribute either to Bradshaw himself, or to the state of his birth. The floors were covered with uneven boards reminiscent of a saloon, and the furniture was all made from finely polished oak. Every one of the chairs was about the size of ones that might be found around an elegant dinner table.

All of the chairs except, of course, the one behind Bradshaw's desk.

That chair was more like a throne. It had a back that was taller and wider than Bradshaw's expansive build and was covered with a thick layer of padded felt. The desk was longer than the arm spans of three men and just under half as deep. Still, the man sitting behind that desk somehow managed to make himself fit behind all that expensive finery as if he'd been born and dropped in that spot.

Shelves lined the walls on either side of the desk and each shelf was filled with various trophies of one kind or another. Those trophies ranged from animals that had been shot and stuffed, to pistols that had been bronzed and mounted.

All in all, Clint couldn't decide which was funnier: that he felt like he was in a museum, or that the museum had been built in honor of Mark Bradshaw.

"Clint Adams!" bellowed a stout man with silver hair who was almost lost behind the mammoth desk. "Long time no see! Get on over here to shake my hand!"

Wincing at the way Bradshaw shouted as if he was talking to Clint across a half mile of open prairie, Clint made the trek across the office until he was able to lean over the desk and shake the other man's hand.

Bradshaw's grip was like iron and he pumped Clint's arm as if he was trying to break it off.

"Where the hell have you been?"

Clint shrugged after reclaiming his arm. "Wherever the wind takes me." Even before he'd said it, Clint knew the words sounded overly dramatic. Still, they were just the type of thing that Bradshaw would love to hear.

Sure enough, the older man's wide face broke into a smile that even lifted his bulbous nose up a half inch or so. His rounded chest swelled out as he dusted off some bits of dust from his expensive gray suit that only he could see. "Still the wandering cowboy, huh? That's splendid! I wish I could drift free as you please without a care in the world."

"I wouldn't build it up quite that way, but it's been interesting." Glancing around at the office and all of its countless decorations, Clint added, "It looks to me like you can go pretty much wherever you like."

Bradshaw dismissed the comment with a wave. "Aw, you know how it goes. The more a man has, the more he's got to keep an eye on it."

Clint knew exactly how that went. That was exactly why he traveled with only as much as he could fit into his saddlebags.

"Glad to see you got my letter," Bradshaw said. "How is ol' Rick doing these days?"

"Prospering just fine," was all Clint said, since he could tell that Bradshaw was just being polite by asking.

"Splendid, splendid."

"Speaking of that letter, it wasn't exactly clear why you wanted me to come out here."

"Long on wind and short on meaning," Bradshaw chuckled. "Is that what yer telling me?"

"Well . . . pretty much."

"Have you gotten a chance to see the town?"

Clint nodded. "I've been here a day or two. You know, just to check the lay of the land."

Snapping his fingers, Bradshaw said, "I knew the moment you rode into town. I just thought I'd let you take yer time, get settled and wait for you to come pay me a visit."

After only this amount of time, Clint was reminded of why it was good to pay Bradshaw a visit maybe once every year or two. Even though he was standing still, the conversation was making Clint feel as if he'd been walking endlessly through a desert of hot air.

"So why'd you send the letter, Mark?" Clint asked, doing his best to cut to the point without seeming too rude.

Dropping down into his padded chair, Bradshaw looked up at a point on the ceiling and held his hands out at arm's length. He gazed through his spread fingers and spoke as if he was addressing the president himself. "Clint Adams, I brought you here to save my town from ruination."

NINE

Clint let Bradshaw take his dramatic pause before he rolled his eyes and sat down in one of the smaller chairs on the other side of the desk. From there, Clint looked the Texan straight in the eyes and said, "Sounds like a whole lot more wind to me."

There was a moment where it seemed that Bradshaw was on the verge of either getting angry or laughing. He chose the latter and broke out into a guffaw so loud that it filled every inch of the office. "Y'see?" Bradshaw said while looking over Clint's shoulder. "This is why I went through so much trouble to find this man."

Clint turned in his chair to get a look at who Bradshaw was talking to. The man who'd shown Clint into the office without saying a word was still standing at the door with his hands clasped in front of him.

The man nodded and smiled, but only until Bradshaw was no longer looking directly at him.

Looking back at Clint, Bradshaw brought a finger to his mustache and ran it along the waxed curl of whiskers. "Have you ever heard of Los Tejanos, Clint?"

"I did once I got about a few day's ride from it."

"Right, because we've got water and food in an area

38

where you need to know where to find such things. What I'm talking about is anything you might have heard the last time you were in New York or California."

"Actually, it's been a while since I've been as far east as New York."

"What about California?" Bradshaw asked, leaning forward and setting both hands flat upon his desk.

"Last time I was there, I had other things to keep me busy instead of gossip about other towns."

Bradshaw smirked and nodded. "I'll just bet you did. And that, my friend, is why I wrote that letter. This town is in some serious trouble."

"It seems pretty quiet to me. I ran into a bit of trouble last night, but it wasn't anything too serious."

Wagging his finger at Clint, the Texan said, "I'm talking about financial trouble. Forget about outlaws or that kind of nonsense. If a town runs out of money, that's when the real trouble happens. That's what turns a fine place to live into a few deserted streets and empty shells behind fading storefronts."

"You paint a good picture," Clint admitted. "But I'm the wrong man to ask if you're looking for a loan or even an investor."

Bradshaw dismissed those words like they were flies buzzing around his head. "I wouldn't presume to ask for anything like that."

"Then I'd appreciate it if you got around to asking for whatever you do want." Taking a breath to control his growing impatience, Clint added, "Not to be rude, but—"

"Poker."

Bradshaw spoke that word as if he'd just invented it on the spot. His eyes were wide and he was gazing up at the ceiling again. His bearing had taken such a turn that Clint half-expected to see a ray of light shine down onto Bradshaw's head.

"Poker?" Clint asked, once he realized that Bradshaw thought his point had been made.

The Texan nodded enthusiastically. "I want to put this town on the map and I think poker is the way to do it."

"You mean to start a tournament?"

"No, nothing so shortsighted. A tournament might bring some folks in for that length of time, but that's only if they know it's being held. What I aim to do is make Los Tejanos a stop on the gambler's circuit. Once that happens, word will spread about us, businesses will prosper and the entire town will grow. Everybody wins that way, Clint."

"Yeah. Especially you."

Although he tried to maintain his visionary posture, Bradshaw allowed himself to smirk knowingly in Clint's direction. "Someone's got to sit at the head of the table, Clint. And it—"

"It might as well be you," Clint said, beating Bradshaw to the punch.

The Texan wasn't used to being cut short. That much was obvious by the way his eyes and nostrils flared for a moment when Clint did just that. Suddenly, he broke out into laughter and slapped the top of his desk so hard that it made everything laying there jump up an inch.

"You got that right, Adams!"

"So what do you want from me?"

"I want you to make the rounds," Bradshaw said, holding his arms out expansively. "Sample the saloons. Play some cards." His eyes narrowed like he was a coyote who'd just spotted a wounded deer. "Play lots of cards."

Clint nodded. "And make sure everyone knows about it."

"Now you're talking!"

Now that he finally knew what was on Bradshaw's mind, Clint felt as if a weight had been lifted from his shoulders. He leaned back in his chair a little and had to resist the urge to put his feet up on the colossal desk.

"That might not be as great an idea as you might think,

you know," Clint said. "Sometimes gamblers aren't the only ones to come out of the woodwork when they know I'm around."

Shrugging, Bradshaw replied, "I own a piece of every saloon in this town, Clint. I won't tolerate any sort of trouble in any of them. Besides, if there are any incidents, I've got boys there that can watch your back."

"I'm not worried about that. It's just that you might not be getting the type of publicity you were after."

"You just play cards, Clint. Have a good time and I'll cover all your expenses. Let me worry about the publicity."

"And you figure this will save your town?" Clint asked.

"It's a start. And once the ball gets rolling, I'll make sure it keeps on rolling until we're as big as Tombstone or even San Francisco."

"Funny you should mention San Francisco," Clint said. "Not too long ago, a saloon owner thought to get some publicity by pulling the very same stunt. There were bills printed and posted all over town."

"I did hear about that," Bradshaw said. "And that's how I know it worked so well."

Although Clint had a few reservations with Bradshaw's logic, it was hard to say no to the Texan. He had a way of pitching deals that was good enough to land him in a luxurious office in the middle of his own town. Besides, the offer being posed wasn't all that bad.

"What the hell," Clint said. "I'm always up for a game of poker."

TEN

Despite the fact that Bradshaw seemed in love with his plans to put Los Tejanos on the map, it was obvious that he didn't like it being known that his idea wasn't entirely original. Clint could tell that much using some of the same skills that had served his so well in so many card games over the years.

Bradshaw had twitched slightly and his fingers curled into a half-fist before he was able to put his confident face back on. That was all Clint needed to see for him to know that there was more going on in the Texan's mind than a few high-stakes games.

Then again, for a man as rich and powerful as Bradshaw, hatching new schemes every other hour was all a part of the game. That was a big reason why Clint preferred to keep his life simple whenever possible. Of course, such a thing was easier said than done, mainly thanks to the schemes and plans of men like Mark Bradshaw.

For the time being, Clint decided to play along and see where events took him. It helped that his normal night's activity had been doing the very thing that Bradshaw had requested of him. For all its other charms, Los Tejanos wasn't exactly a hub of activity.

There wasn't much else to do apart from tour the saloons. The only difference now was that Clint could drop a name and get his evening paid for. That was well worth signing on to Bradshaw's plan to bring some new life into the town.

Then again, all Clint had to do was think about that for a moment for a weary smile to cross his face.

The first saloon he found was a place called Billy Bob's. It didn't seem like much, but Clint had to test a theory of his before heading to some of the bigger places farther down the street. Folks were out and about in force by this time, filling the streets and boardwalks as they tended to their daily business.

Carts ambled down the wider streets and every storefront was open for business. Smiles were present on shopkeepers' faces as Clint walked by, beckoning for him to come in and spend a bit of his money. But the storefront where Clint was headed didn't seem quite so welcoming.

On the contrary, Billy Bob's was empty and the door was only open because the heat had warped the boards to keep it from shutting properly. Clint pushed the door open and stepped inside, immediately smelling the stale leftover scents of last night's tobacco smoke and cheap liquor.

"We're closing up," a man at the back of the room said. "Come back after we're done cleaning the place."

"You the owner?" Clint asked.

The man studied him for a moment and then put on an aggravated expression. "Yeah, and I'm also the one that told you to clear out. If you don't take that advice, you won't be welcome here when we do open up."

Clint looked around at the card tables set up in the back of the room, the little, empty stage beside a vacant piano and then the bar that stretched from one end of the saloon to the other. Just then, stripped down to the bare bones like that, Billy Bob's looked like every other saloon in every other town that Clint had ever visited.

Something else seemed familiar as well. In fact, Clint was surprised it had taken him this long to sniff it out.

The owner was still eyeing Clint suspiciously and working his way to the bar. Surely, he meant to replace the broom in his hands with something a bit more deadly.

"My name's Clint Adams. I was told to expect better treatment than this."

That changed the owner's expression completely. Now, rather than looking annoyed, he was about to trip over himself to get close enough to shake Clint's hand.

"Yer Clint Adams? I didn't know you were here yet." With a sheepish grin, he added, "Mr. Bradshaw told us to expect you, but most of us didn't think he could get someone like you to show."

"So Mr. Bradshaw told you I was coming?"

"Certainly."

"And what did he say besides that?"

"Just to treat you right and make sure you didn't have to pay for a single thing. Can I get you a drink, Mr. Adams?"

Clint rolled his eyes and shook his head. "No thanks. I already got what I was after."

ELEVEN

This time, when Clint walked through Bradshaw's office, he wasn't looking at the furniture or extravagant decorations. He barely even spared a glance toward the men outside Bradshaw's door who tried to stop him and ask what business he had with the rich Texan inside.

Clint walked right past them, right past all the big chairs and numerous shelves until he was face-to-face with Bradshaw once again. By the time he got there, even Bradshaw himself looked like he couldn't believe what he was seeing.

"Clint, I didn't think I'd—" Bradshaw started to say.

Clint cut him off with a voice that was sharper than any blade. "Yeah? And I didn't think I'd be signed up to do a job before I accepted it."

For a moment, Bradshaw tried to look surprised. He cut that act the moment he saw that it was only making Clint even madder. "If you said no, I wouldn't have expected anything else from you," he said earnestly.

"That's not the point." Clint took a breath and eased himself down into the same chair where he'd been sitting before. "It seems to me that no matter where I go, someone's got a job for me. And no matter what I may think or what I may try, those same people always figure I'll do whatever job they have in mind."

"Must be rough to be in such high demand."

Clint picked up on the sarcasm in Bradshaw's voice, but also felt a joking tone that almost brought a smile to his face. "Look, Bradshaw, you helped out Rick when he needed it and I truly appreciate it. I wouldn't mind helping you out if it was something really important, but when every saloon owner in town already knows I've taken on a job before I even accepted it, that shows me that I'm being taken for granted.

"Friends help each other out, but this is like you're ordering me to do a service and the thought that I might refuse isn't even a possibility. That's not treating someone like a friend. It's treating them like an employee."

Bradshaw had been starting to say something, but stopped himself and took a moment to think. Just when it seemed that he was going to launch himself into another sales pitch, the Texan let out his breath and slumped as though all the wind had been taken from him. "You're right, Clint."

That had been the last thing Clint had expected the man to say.

"But," Bradshaw continued, "as long as you're here, why not stay awhile as my guest? As far as the offer I made about you drinking for free, that still goes. From one friend to another." Bradshaw stepped around his desk so he could stand next to Clint. "Ol' Rick's helped me out plenty over the years, so think of this as my way of extending a courtesy."

Clint watched Bradshaw for a bit before finally realizing that the Texan wasn't joking.

"Of course, if you change your mind about the original offer, I'd certainly appreciate it."

That little bit of callousness was enough to prove to

Clint that Bradshaw was being genuine. Rather than make him mad, it made Clint laugh and shake his head.

"Tell you what, Bradshaw. I'll let you in on something, from one friend to another. I go to plenty of saloons and have met plenty of owners trying to make their places the best of the bunch. They all want to cater to gamblers and get these big reputations from gunfighters, but you know what none of them really think to do?"

Bradshaw had already sat down on the edge of his desk and was listening intently. "What's that?"

"Not one of them buys a gambler a drink and asks them what type of place they'd like to see."

"I always figured that that would mean taking on another partner to get that kind of information."

"Well," Clint said as he got up and looked Bradshaw square in the eye. "That's where having a friend like me really comes in handy, isn't it?"

"Well, if you wouldn't mind, I would certainly appreciate your advice of what you think I might be able to do to bring some more business into this town. I'm not just talking about the saloons, either. I'm talking businesses and even a train station."

"Let's just take it one step at a time. To be perfectly honest, I think you'll do just fine on your own."

When Clint stood up, he wasn't feeling a fraction of the anger that had brought him storming into the office. The main thing on his mind was why everyone thought they could use him as a way to get rich, get famous or both.

Maybe if he could figure that out, he could think of a way to make himself rich. Then again, doing that would take away from everything that he truly enjoyed in his life.

"How about we meet up again tonight?" Bradshaw asked. "I can take you around to see all the places I'm looking to improve and you can give me your thoughts.

Maybe you can even tell me about how they do it in some of the better places you've seen."

"Sounds good. I'll come by here later on."

Bradshaw slapped Clint's back and put on a smile that was almost wider than his entire head. "I'm lookin' forward to it, Clint. You know where to find me."

Clint nodded and made his way out of the office. Before he was out of the room, he could hear Bradshaw calling in his assistants and going over some other kind of strategy for some other type of plan. Clint didn't bother trying to figure out what the plan involved, because he felt like he'd already wasted too much time. Once he was on the street again, he was looking at Los Tejanos in a new way.

Bradshaw had gotten him to start thinking of things from a business perspective and Clint wasn't sure if he should be mad about that or not. In the end, he decided that the Texan was catching a few bills for him, so he might as well help Bradshaw out. At the very least, Clint owed it to Rick to do that much at least.

He was passing the Second Chance Saloon when another thought hit him. There was someone else in town who needed help a whole lot more than Mark Bradshaw. Before he took one more step, Clint walked into Bradshaw's office for a third time just so he could ask one more question.

"Who's Boyle Gilliam?"

TWELVE

Boyle Gilliam set up his own office in the upper floor of Rosie's Gentleman's Club. Rosie's was one of the worst kept secrets in town by being one of the most well-known cathouses in the county. But just because everyone knew what Rosie's was, that didn't mean that the place didn't go through the motions of keeping itself hidden.

The outside of the building was well maintained and covered in dark wood paneling. Each window was covered by dark green shades or curtains while each door was fitted with a polished brass handle. Inside, the main floor was a dimly lit collection of felt covered tables used for either playing cards or entertaining with drinks.

A talented piano player filled the air with subdued music, which acted as a nice companion to the low, baritone rumble of conversation. The men doing the talking were mostly refined types with full heads of perfectly groomed hair. There were plenty of other types mixed in as well, but even they conducted themselves like gentlemen. If they didn't, they wouldn't be allowed to go upstairs to sample Rosie's specialty.

The upstairs rooms were even nicer than the downstairs and it had nothing to do with the carpeting or furnishings.

The best scenery in town was upstairs at Rosie's and that scenery consisted mainly of scantily clad women lounging about, waiting for their next customer.

Rosie herself had an office up there, and in the back of that office was a narrow staircase leading up to what should have been nothing but an attic. That attic was another fully furnished office that might have even put Bradshaw's to shame if he had more space to work with.

There were paintings on the walls and a few nicely padded chairs to match the desk built from polished mahogany. The only window in the room was a large round one on the opposite side from the desk overlooking one of the busier streets in town. Standing in front of that window was a tall man with broad shoulders wearing a dark, pinstriped suit.

That man looked to be in his late fifties. He stood well over six feet tall and had a head of thick, gray hair. His skin was olive hued and leathery, creased with enough wrinkles to mark nearly every expression his face had ever worn.

"Is that who I think it is?" the man asked in a deep, rasping voice.

Another man stepped up to stand at the window beside him. Looking down at the street below, the younger man smirked and said, "I'll be damned. I think it is, Mr. Gilliam."

The man standing next to Gilliam was dressed as if he was doing his best to emulate his boss. Although he wore a suit as well, he didn't have the bearing to go along with it. Instead, he stood like a cowhand leaning against a hitching post and being in the most expensive suit in the world wouldn't have changed a thing.

Like everyone else in the room, the younger man was armed. He wore his pistol in plain view, strapped around his waist in an expensive holster. Mr. Gilliam was a bit more subtle, preferring to wear his guns in a shoulder holster that fit perfectly beneath his tailored suit jacket.

"And here I thought I was going to have to send out Danny Boy to have a talk with that unlucky son of a bitch," Gilliam said. "What do you think, boys? Has ol' Wilbur come into some money and is on his way to pay me off?"

All of the other men standing or sitting in the office grumbled some sort of response, but Gilliam wasn't really listening. His eyes were planted firmly on Wilbur Johanssen who was making his way across the street at that very moment. In fact, Wilbur almost got run over by a wagon before he made it to Rosie's front door.

Gilliam shook his head and smiled. There wasn't the slightest trace of affection in that smile. Instead, he looked amused at almost seeing Wilbur get run down. There was a definite sparkle in his eyes that showed how much wider he would have smiled if that wagon had found its mark.

"Where is Danny Boy, anyway?" Gilliam asked.

"He's out on that errand."

"Which errand?"

"The one he told you about earlier."

Gilliam thought for a moment and then nodded. "Oh, that's right. Did he need any of that information he was after?"

"Nah. Turned out that all he needed to do was ask one of the saloon keepers on Fourth Street."

"Good," Gilliam said in a voice that rumbled at the back of his throat.

Wilbur had pulled open the door and just managed to step aside before he was knocked over by a pair of men swaggering outside after their time upstairs. Although Wilbur shot a hard look at the two, it wasn't until the other men were well away from him. After that, he was able to step inside and out of Gilliam's field of vision.

Turning his back to the window, Gilliam walked over to his desk and sat on the edge. He twisted around to take a cigarette from a gold case that had been laying there and fitted it into the corner of his mouth. "One of you boys get down there," he said, every syllable causing the cigarette to jump and wobble. "Make sure that Wilbur finds his way up here."

One of the men who'd been sitting in a chair closest to the door stood up and straightened his suit jacket. The way he did so made it painfully obvious that dressing so formally was a very new thing to him. "I'll do it, Mr. Gilliam. I was about to head down there anyway."

Gilliam watched as the man did his best to straighten himself up before leaving the room. With a subtle nod, he got another of the gunmen in the room to stand up and join the first.

With his had still poised on the door, the man looked back to Gilliam and asked, "What should I do if he's not here to see you?"

"Convince him," Gilliam replied. "Convince him until he bleeds."

THIRTEEN

Wilbur Johanssen was all too familiar with Rosie's Gentleman's Club even though he'd never sampled much of what it had to offer. He usually had less enjoyable business to take care of when he was there and, all too often, he was being dragged inside while in some state of bloody disarray.

This time, although he was moving on his own steam, Wilbur felt like he was being pulled in by a noose. His head was kept angled downward and his hands were thrust deeply into his pockets. He even flinched at every noise he heard that was louder than a boot crunching against gravel in the street.

When that crunching approached him directly, however, Wilbur braced himself for the worst.

"Hey Wilbur," a voice said from directly behind him. "What are you doing here?"

Shifting around timidly at first, Wilbur let out a relieved breath when he saw who'd addressed him. "Mister Adams. I didn't expect to see you so soon."

Clint smiled and took a look around to make sure that he'd come to the right place. "And I certainly didn't expect to find you around here, either. Aren't you a married man?"

Reflexively, Wilbur checked the scraped spot around his

left finger. Even though he knew it was going to be empty the space still made his stomach pull tightly into a knot. "Yeah. I'm married."

"Then what are you doing outside a gentleman's club?"

Wilbur straightened up and tried to put a casual smile onto his face. He wasn't very successful. "Are you saying I'm not a gentleman?"

"No. I'm saying that you're not the type to walk into a cathouse. Even if it's a cathouse as finely dressed up as this one."

Wilbur shrugged and tried to come up with something to say to Clint. Before anything came to mind, however, he heard the door to Rosie's get pushed open and a series of heavy steps pound against the boardwalk. The voice that followed was even more familiar than Clint's. Unfortunately, it wasn't half as welcome.

"Howdy, Wilbur," Bradshaw's gunman said while strutting outside. Even though he still didn't look anywhere close to being comfortable in his suit, he seemed right at home when spitting his words out to Wilbur. "A little early in the day to dip yer wick, ain't it?"

"I'm not here for that," Wilbur said. "I just wanted to see about making an arrangement with Mr. Gilliam."

Just then, the door opened again to allow another man to step outside. This one was also dressed in a fancy suit, although he looked to be a little more at ease in it. "Yeah?" this second man asked as he pulled aside his jacket to show the gun strapped around his waist. "Well maybe Mr. Gilliam is sick of dealing with sorry dirt farmers like yourself."

Clint could read the intentions of the two gunmen as clearly as if they'd been written across their faces. Both of them looked at Wilbur like they were already planning on where they were going to leave him when they got done ripping him apart.

"There's no need for this," Wilbur said. "I brought some money. It's all I could scrape up. I just want my ring back."

"Your ring?" the first gunman asked. "Whatever you're talking about, it ain't no concern of ours."

"My wedding ring. O'Shea took it from me."

That brought a grim smile to both of the gunmen's faces. It was the second one who nodded as he said, "That's right. Danny Boy was telling me about that. He says he'd make a better husband than you. Actually, I've seen yer wife and I think I'd make a pretty good suitor, too. Maybe Danny'll let me borrow that ring for a night or two."

Wilbur's fists tightened and he bit down hard upon the bait that had been dangled in front of him by the other two. Just as he was about to make a big mistake, Clint stopped him by taking hold of his shoulder and stepping forward.

"How much does he owe you?" Clint asked.

The other two men glared at him as if they'd just noticed him standing there.

"And who the hell are you?" the second one asked.

Clint not only met the gunman's gaze, but put enough fire into his own eyes to back him up a step. "I'm the man that just asked you a question. How much?"

The first gunman snapped his suit jacket open before pulling it completely off so he could show the double rig around his waist. Only then did he look like he wasn't a kid squirming in Sunday school. "He owes Mr. Gilliam two thousand dollars."

"Fifteen hundred," Wilbur spoke up.

The first gunman gritted his teeth in a vicious snarl and snapped his left arm straight out to backhand Wilbur across the face. His strike was quick as a whip, which made it all the more impressive when Clint was able to snatch him by the wrist a few inches short of his intended target.

Keeping hold of the gunman's wrist, Clint came forward even more until he was standing toe-to-toe with him.

His eyes held so much intensity that when he stared the younger man down, it seemed as though Clint could look all the way through to the back of his skull.

"Wilbur," Clint said without taking his eyes off of the man in front of him, "how much money did you bring?"

It took a moment for Wilbur to collect himself, but he eventually replied, "T . . . two hundred."

"Give it to me."

Clint's other hand was stretched out behind him and was soon filled by a wad of folded bills. Without looking at the money, Clint stuffed the bills into the gunman's shirt pocket. "Here," he said. "This should be enough to get the ring back. Now go fetch it for him."

The gunman was already shaking his head. Although he was smiling, his eyes were twitching wildly. Just then, his left hand darted down to snatch one of his guns from the holster in a movement that was even quicker than when he'd tried to smack Wilbur.

Just as before, Clint was a bit quicker.

Having managed to let go of the gunman's wrist, reach for his modified Colt and clear leather in the blink of an eye, Clint stuck the pistol's barrel into the younger man's gut.

"Draw," Clint said with a grin.

FOURTEEN

For a moment, the gunman didn't even realize his situation. He felt the iron wedged into his stomach, but couldn't quite believe that Clint had managed to clear leather. One quick look downward was all he needed to clear that up and when he saw the Colt in his gut, he had to look one more time just to be certain.

"You've got your payment," Clint said. "There's no need for this to get any uglier."

The second gunman shifted from one foot to the other. His eyes darted between Clint, his partner, Wilbur and a few others who'd stopped what they were doing to see what was going on. His hand hovered over his own pistol, but wasn't sure enough of himself to do any more than that.

"But he still owes Mr. Gilliam," the first gunman managed to say. "He still owes plenty."

"Nobody's saying any different," Clint said. "All I'm saying is that there's no need for any more unpleasantness when Mr. Johanssen is here to make a payment. I'd say that since his ring was stolen from him as a punishment for being late, it should be returned now that he's done his part."

"That ring stays right where it is," the second gunman said after finding enough gumption to do so.

Now that he was reminded of his backup, the first gunman straightened up despite the Colt in his belly. "Yeah. Whatever Wilbur paid you to step in for him, it wasn't enough to make up for all the hell that's headed your way if you keep it up."

Clint didn't say a word to that.

In fact, the longer he remained silent, the quieter everything else around him seemed to get.

Neither of the gunmen were making a sound.

Nobody watching the scene dared to speak.

Even the wind seemed to fall still with every moment that passed.

Finally, Clint made a motion that was so quick, it seemed to come from out of nowhere. He backed up a step and slid the modified Colt back into its holster in such a fast couple of motions that it caused both gunmen to react as though they were under attack. When the first gunman flinched, he didn't immediately realize that his wrist was no longer being held.

Clint took another step back, but didn't take his eyes off of the man in front of him. "All right then," he said calmly. "I've got a proposition for you. I'll take on Wilbur's debt, your Mr. Gilliam will get his money and this whole mess goes away."

"And in return?" the second gunman asked suspiciously.

"In return, Mr. Johanssen gets his life and his wedding ring back."

The first gunman looked over to his partner as though he was waiting for the second shoe to drop. When it didn't, he didn't seem to know quite what to do.

All this time, while his partner had been getting riled up and Clint had been forced to put him in his place, the second gunman had remained calm. That was enough to draw Clint's attention to him, as it most certainly meant he was the more experienced of the two.

"And what if we refuse?" the second gunman asked. "What then?"

Clint shrugged. "I'm not throwing down any threats or giving ultimatums. I'm making you an offer and I don't see any reason why someone would refuse it."

"That's a lot of money you're talking about."

"I know."

"And where'd you get it?" the first gunman asked.

"Does it matter? I'm good for it. That's all you need to know."

Just when the first gunman was getting ready to spit out a particularly nasty reply to Clint's offer, he was cut short by the level baritone of the second man's voice.

"We can let Mr. Gilliam know about it and see what he says."

Reflexively, the first gunman glanced back and up to the topmost window of the gentleman's club. Clint looked in that direction as well and spotted the imposing figure filling up most of the round window on that floor.

Clint didn't have to be told who was standing in that window. The man gazed down at the street with sharp eyes and a demeanor that could be felt even through the glass pane and the distance between them. From the sharp angle of where he was standing, Clint couldn't make out details, but the authority in that man's face was plain enough.

That had to be Mr. Gilliam.

Either that, or Los Tejanos had an emperor that Clint hadn't known about.

FIFTEEN

"Come on, Jack," the second gunman said. "Let's go up and see what Mr. Gilliam thinks about this offer."

Although Jack didn't look too happy about it, he was more than willing to put some distance between himself and Clint. Before he took a step toward Rosie's door, however, he took one more glance up at Gilliam's window.

The silver-haired man was not pleased. That much was painfully obvious by the scowl that had been etched onto his face since the last time Jack had looked up there.

The second gunman hadn't turned his back on Clint, but was in the process of walking up the stairs. He moved with an easy confidence, but still managed to keep his hands within an inch or so of his holster.

Jack, on the other hand, wasn't inclined to go back into Rosie's so easily. "Aw, to hell with this. Mr. Gilliam said we were to bring that asshole upstairs to have a talk with him," he grunted, jabbing a finger toward Wilbur.

"This ain't the time to make a scene," the second gunman warned. Before he could say another word, things had already been steered in the wrong direction.

Jack came steaming forward like a dog that was eager to impress its master. His hands were both going down toward his guns and his eyes were firmly set on Wilbur. At the last moment, he snapped his gaze over in Clint's direction and lashed out with the same fist that Clint had already caught once before.

With his attention divided between four different people now, Clint was on the lookout for anyone to reach for their guns. Even the man in the window or Wilbur were potential threats since they could send things to hell just as easily with a bad enough move.

That was the only reason that Jack was able to sneak in his quick jab before Clint could duck out of the way. His eyes were searching for iron and only saw the incoming fist when it was too late.

Jack's punch snapped out like a whip, coming in even faster now that it wasn't wrapped around a pistol. His knuckles caught Clint on the jaw and snapped his head around to one side.

Catching the punch from the younger man brought up Clint's ire right away. Seeing the cocky grin on Jack's face stoked Clint's fires even more. Luckily, Jack was still plenty willing to give him an opportunity to pay back that punch with interest.

"How'd you like that?" Jack sneered. "I'll bet you'll like this even more!"

Now that he was watching Jack closer, Clint could see the younger man's movements coming like they'd been written and sent via telegraph. Jack shifted his weight while moving forward. His right arm cocked back as he snapped out with the left in a slow, waggling punch.

Allowing the feinting punch to bounce off of him, Clint prepared himself for the real blow to come from Jack's right hand. Sure enough, he didn't have to wait long at all before that right arm swung out to deliver a powerful hook.

Holding out his left arm, Clint blocked the punch while twisting his hand open and around to grab hold of whatever he could. His fingers closed around Jack's forearm, but not before Jack started pulling it back in an attempt to break free.

All Jack succeeded in doing was presenting Clint with something he could lock around even better: the same wrist that had been locked up before. Clint's grip sealed up nicely in that same spot, allowing him to pull Jack toward him and into a straight right punch of his own.

Clint's fist had plenty of steam behind it as it was, but that combined with Jack's momentum to create a jarring impact that nearly took the younger man's head clean off his shoulders. Jack's chin snapped back and his knees buckled beneath him. For a moment, Clint's grasp was the only thing keeping him up. In the next moment, Jack was filled with more than enough fury to pull himself free of that same grip.

"Goddammit," the second gunman grumbled as he reluctantly threw himself into the very scuffle he'd been hoping to avoid.

SIXTEEN

The second gunman had been hanging back far enough until now, but all of that was set to change. Since he couldn't set the fight up the way he wanted, he joined in with every intention of winning. His hands closed into thick fists and he waded into the brawl as though he feared neither man nor beast.

Clint had been keeping an eye on the second gunman and saw him coming forward like a rolling log. Just as he was about to do something about it, he saw another flash of movement from a source he hadn't expected.

Although Wilbur wasn't as sure of himself as the other fighters, he entered the fray all the same. Both hands were clenched into fists and his eyes were wide with an equal mix of fear and dread.

Still reeling from the punch he'd recently taken, Jack found himself within an arm's reach of Wilbur and took full advantage of it. His left hand snapped out with a quick jab that clipped Wilbur's cheek. Just as he was about to follow up with an uppercut, he felt something akin to a slab of wood pound against his chest and drive him back.

That slab was Clint's hand as it connected with Jack before the man could do any real damage to Wilbur.

For the moment, Clint had as much control as could be expected in the situation. He'd put his back to the street and had all of his opponents in sight. That still left plenty of room for things to go wrong, but the trick to surviving any kind of fight was to focus on what you could do, rather than every other possibility.

His next concern was the second gunman who was still charging at him with increasing momentum. It looked like there wasn't going to be a way around taking at least one punch from the gunman, so Clint braced himself for the impact.

It never came.

Instead, Clint heard the sound of another impact as Wilbur literally threw himself at the second gunman. The normally timid man had worked himself into enough of a lather to follow up his charge with a flurry of punches. Unfortunately, that flurry was all too short-lived.

The gunman absorbed a few blows, but drove his fist deep into Wilbur's gut. Not only did the punch land just right, but Wilbur's body seemed to fold in around it as every bit of air was forced from his lungs.

When he turned to look at Clint, the second gunman still had Wilbur hanging from his fist like a slab of meat. That made it impossible for him to do much when he was greeted by the sight of Jack's bloodied face bouncing against the street and Clint walking straight toward him.

Suddenly, the air exploded with the distinct roar of a shotgun's blast.

Everyone stopped what they were doing.

Fists froze in midswing. Curses went half-said. Even folks standing around on the street ducked part of the way before their muscles just refused to move anymore.

"All right, all right," said a short, stocky woman standing in the doorway to Rosie's. "This has gone on plenty far enough."

The woman wore a mix of layers that ranged from formal all the way down to sleazy. Her petticoats were hanging at odd angles from her shoulders, arms and breasts without revealing more than a few inches of actual skin. Her skinny legs were wrapped up in boots that covered up the tattered stockings underneath them.

Her face looked as though it had been pretty several years ago, but was now pinched and wrinkled into a cantankerous mask. Her mouth came in just tightly enough to make it obvious that she had few, if any, remaining teeth. Short, dark red hair stuck out from beneath the brim of a large, expensive hat.

Although her eyes were fierce and sharp enough to command respect, the smoking shotgun in her hands was enough to give her even more authority over the men fighting in front of the club.

"Don't you boys have enough to keep you busy inside my place?" she asked. "Or would you rather knock each other around than let one of my girls get their hands on you?"

Jack spat out a mix of blood and saliva before saying, "Point that gun somewhere else, Kathy! This don't concern you."

"No," came a voice from within the club. The man who'd just spoken put his hand on Kathy's shoulder and politely moved her aside so he could step past her. He was the same man that had just been standing in the uppermost window only a minute ago. "But it does concern me."

SEVENTEEN

Grudgingly, Jack held his tongue and fully allowed himself to lower his guard. Even though he'd been locked in a fight with Clint, he all but forgot about that as he walked up to stand beside the well-dressed figure.

The second gunman didn't defer so drastically. Then again, he hadn't thrown himself into the fight as much as his partner in the first place. He merely bowed his head slightly and stepped off once he saw that Clint wasn't about to take advantage of the current state of calm.

Still breathing heavily from the fight, Clint could feel his blood surging through his veins. It was jarring to be pulled from the fray like that, but he was more than willing to put an end to the brawl. Clint's eyes shifted between the two gunmen. Although he was certain their leashes had been pulled hard enough to make them stop, he wasn't about to bet his life on that.

"I apologize on behalf on my boys here," the silver-haired man said. "Please, accept my offer for a drink. It's the least I can do to make up for this obvious misunderstanding."

"Misunderstanding?" Clint asked. "Is that what you call it?"

The man shrugged. "For lack of a better term. I'm sure we can straighten it out inside. At least we'll be off the street."

Clint looked around and saw that a sizeable crowd had gathered around them. There were more people joining the group every second, obviously attracted by the commotion of the scuffle and the shotgun blast. Another thing that was obvious was that the silver-haired man didn't like being under such close scrutiny.

"I'll keep an eye out for you," the man said. And, making eye contact with Wilbur, he added, "Both of you."

With that, the silver-haired man snapped his fingers and turned to walk back into the club. Jack grumbled something under his breath while taking one more look at Clint, but followed closely on the man's heels.

The second gunman didn't seem to be affected by much of anything around him. His focus remained on Clint and Wilbur, the way a wolf's focus remained fixed upon the throat it most wanted to tear open. Even so, he still knew where his orders came from. After a subtle nod to Clint, he walked past Kathy and entered the club.

"You heard the man," Kathy said as she cradled the shotgun in her arm like a baby. "Just a misunderstanding. Everything turns out for the best at Rosie's!" Even with the shotgun smoke still hanging around her and the blood still in the street, she managed to sound like the whole fight was a show and she was the grand finale.

At the very least, most of the crowd bought in to that same casual feel and got back to whatever they'd originally been doing.

Clint allowed himself to take a deep breath and reach a hand up to touch a spot on his face that still ached from being punched. He winced a bit as the dull pain shot through him. Now that he wasn't more concerned with getting knocked onto his ass, all the bumps and bruises were making themselves known.

"We've got to stop meeting like this, Wilbur," Clint joked.

Although he'd taken his share of hits, Wilbur managed to put a smile onto his face. That sent a jolt through him and he winced, but kept his smirk intact. He sat down onto the edge of the boardwalk and was more than willing to put his feet in the ditch. "Folks always told me that I didn't have no luck at all. I guess you can see why."

"This doesn't have anything to do with luck," Clint replied as he sat down next to Wilbur. "It's got to do with someone throwing his weight around a bit too much."

Wilbur shook his head. "I brought this on myself, Clint. I gambled my money away, borrowed some more and then lost that, too. It's my fault." Rubbing the empty spot on his ring finger, he lowered his head and pushed his boot a little deeper into the muck of the ditch beside the road. "All my fault."

"Maybe to start off," Clint said. "But there's a limit to everything. You've got your debts, but that doesn't make it right for someone to collect them in blood. Especially when you mean to pay them off."

Wilbur looked over at him and studied Clint for a moment. In a weary voice, he said, "You barely even know me. I'm just a gambler, and a bad one at that. Why do you think someone like me deserves to be treated any better than this?"

"Because I'm a good gambler," Clint said. "And part of that is because I can size others up fairly well." After taking a moment to do just that, Clint convinced himself that he'd picked the right side in this fight.

The harder part was in deciding that he wanted any part of the fight at all. But he'd decided that much before even setting his eyes upon Rosie's Gentleman's Club.

Mark Bradshaw was a rich man with enough brains to think of plenty of ways to solve his little dilemma. Wilbur Johanssen, on the other hand, was a hard-luck case who was dangerously close to being stomped into the muck even deeper than he was stomping his boot at that moment.

Wilbur was the type of man who would never think to ask for help from a man like Clint Adams. For that reason alone, Clint wanted to see that Wilbur got the help he needed before he lost a whole lot more than just his wedding ring.

"Go on home, Wilbur," Clint said.

"But, I need to talk to Mr. Gilliam."

"That's why I came here. Actually, running into you was just a little bonus." Rubbing the bruise on his jaw, Clint added, "A painful bonus, but there isn't much to be done about that now."

"You've done more than enough already," Wilbur said while getting up and brushing himself off. "I mean to go in there and—"

"And what?" Clint interrupted. "Get yourself killed? I don't know what you saw happening out here, but those men were out here for a reason and they weren't stopped until things got out of hand and started drawing too much attention."

The fear in Wilbur's eyes was plain enough to see. But there was also a determination there that Clint had to admire.

"You'll get your chance to talk to Mr. Gilliam," Clint said assuredly. "But I've got something to say to him first. Besides, I'm the one he invited in there to have a drink."

"Actually, he said for both of us to—"

"You need to talk to your wife."

"I do?"

"Yep. You need to tell her you love her and that it's high time you two spent a night in a comfortable room in the nicest hotel in town."

"But, I don't—"

Clint's hand was already in his pocket and removing a few dollars to hand over to Wilbur. "And don't forget to mention that it's a gift from me. After all, if I wasn't here, you would have gotten your nice little chat with Mr. Gilliam without all the punches being thrown."

While that might have been true, Clint figured that Wilbur's quiet little chat would have had a much bloodier outcome if it had been conducted behind closed doors. He didn't mention that and, judging by the somber look in Wilbur's eyes, it didn't really need to be said.

"It's the least I can do, Wilbur. Just take the money."

"But . . . why?"

"Do those men know where you live?"

Wilbur nodded.

"That's why," Clint said. "You need to pack your things and take your wife out of there for a little while. Men like that tend to get their minds set on finishing a fight once it gets started. This scuffle may be over for now, but the fight's got a ways to go yet."

"So what then? I can't hide forever." Straightening up a bit and lifting his chin, Wilbur added, "I won't do that."

"Nobody's asking you to run away. You just need to get yourself and your wife somewhere safe. I don't know this Gilliam fellow too well, but I sure as hell didn't like the look on that younger kid's face who was itching to get out of that suit. He's the type who wouldn't be satisfied with the blood that was spilled here."

There were people walking down the street, but most of them seemed content to go right by Clint and Wilbur. In fact, it seemed that most of them were used to pretending that Rosie's wasn't really there in the first place.

"I'm staying at the Comfort Arms Hotel," Clint said. "You know where that is?"

"Sure I do."

"Then leave word for me there telling me where you and your wife are staying." Suddenly, Clint got a bad feeling. "Do you have any kids?"

"No. Well, not yet anyway."

That was a relief, since keeping two people safe was challenge enough. Worrying about young ones would have only made the situation a whole lot worse. "All right, then. Leave me a note and I'll meet up with you before too long."

Wilbur watched as Clint stood up and started walking toward the front door of the gentleman's club. "What do you intend to do in there?"

Clint could hear the trepidation in the man's voice, as well as the nervous glances directed toward the modified Colt strapped around his waist. "I intend to have a talk and maybe a drink," Clint said. "I'm too damn tired to do much else."

"When I asked you why you were doing this, I didn't just mean the money for the hotel. I meant . . . well . . . why you were doing any of it. Why would you go through all this trouble to help out someone like me? You hardly even know me."

"Let's just say that you caught me in a generous mood," Clint told him. With that, he patted Wilbur on the shoulder and walked into Rosie's. As he walked, Clint waited to hear the sounds of Wilbur making his own departure. Since he wanted to know that the other man was safely out of sight before going any farther, Clint stopped and took one more look over his shoulder.

Wilbur was on his feet, but standing in place with his arms hanging at his sides. When he saw that Clint had stopped, Wilbur said, "I'm not worth all this fuss, Clint."

"I think you are," Clint replied. "Just don't prove me wrong."

EIGHTEEN

Although Clint did get some wary glances from some of the people inside Rosie's, those were far outnumbered by those who either welcomed him or didn't even notice his entrance. Seeing as how punches had been thrown and gunshots fired only moments ago outside the club's doors, that apathy said a lot about Rosie's clientele.

For the most part, the people inside the club were well-dressed men. They were scattered about the foyer and adjoining parlor, sitting in leather padded chairs or leaning against polished bars. Cigar smoke hung in the air, mixed with the scent of expensive pipe tobacco. None of it was too overpowering and all of it went just fine with the vaguely British feel of the room.

The women that were in the parlor bore not even the slightest resemblance to Kathy. Unlike the older woman with the shotgun, the younger ones were dressed in the latest fashions and carried themselves with the smug confidence of knowing that they could get any little thing they wanted.

Kathy stuck out like an even bigger sore thumb when she came walking by those ladies with her shotgun still cradled in her arm. She batted her eyes at Clint like she was the finest in the bunch, however, and set the shotgun down like it was a fine parasol.

"Can I get you a drink, handsome?" she asked.

"Just some water, if it's not too much trouble."

"For you," Kathy said with a wink, "nothing's too much trouble. Nothing at all."

Clint could hear heavier footsteps coming from the next room and didn't have to be told that they belonged to one of the less accommodating people within the club. He could feel the gunman's eyes on him, but refused to give in to the pressure of that gaze. Instead, Clint took his time and waited for his water.

It seemed that Kathy wasn't in much of a hurry, either. She returned with the water, strolling through the club without a care in the world. "Here you go," she said. "If you'd like some company for your next drink, just let me know."

"Would you pawn me off on somebody else or take care of me yourself?"

Kathy blushed and swatted Clint's elbow playfully. "Don't flatter yourself, cowboy. I may be a bit too much for you to handle."

"I'll take your word for it."

Just then, another man wearing a gun stepped into the room. Clint didn't recognize his face, but the fancy suit wrapped around the hired muscle might as well have been a uniform. "If you two are finished," the gunman said, "maybe we can get back to business."

Clint lifted his glass to Kathy and got a wide, albeit somewhat crooked, smile in return. After downing the water, Clint followed the lead of the impatient gunman who was still waiting for him.

While he was being led by the gunman, Clint got a short tour of the gentleman's club as well. The place was done up very nicely. In fact, until he got to the second floor, Clint might have thought that the place truly was just a

place for gentlemen to lounge around, drink and play some
cards.

That impression turned right around the moment Clint
reached the top of the stairs.

Once on the second floor, every one of Clint's senses
were treated to the gentle touch of women. The lighting
and colors all around him became softer and more subdued. The carpeting beneath his feet was thicker and the
walls were covered in a velvet paper.

Flowers adorned every small table in sight, filling the
air with a scent that mingled perfectly with that of perfume. As he walked down the hall, Clint could hear various
conversations taking place. They were intermixed with the
soft sound of laughter, all of which was done by delicate
feminine voices.

The topper of all of that, however, came when Clint
got a look at the women themselves. They sat or stood all
over the second floor, which was made up to look like a
smaller and more intimate version of the downstairs
lounge.

Women of all shapes, colors and sizes were in that
room. Every one of them was dressed in expensive silks
and satins and every one of them gave Clint an inviting
look as he walked by. There were a few gentlemen up
there, but they were outnumbered by the ladies at least
three to one.

The more he saw of the upstairs lounge, the bigger Clint
figured it was. The room just seemed to keep going down
one hallway and another until it eventually branched off
into several private rooms. Clint figured that those rooms
were the destination of most of the men who found their
way up those stairs. Judging by the muffled sound of
voices coming from behind a few of those doors, that assumption was absolutely correct.

More than once, Clint found himself distracted by the
sights and scents all around him. It wasn't so much that the

women were exquisite beauties, but they carried themselves as if they were goddesses. That attitude went a long way, making it easy for Clint to figure out how Rosie could afford all the fancy furniture.

"Time for that later," the gunman said as he tried to recapture Clint's attention. "Mr. Gilliam's office is this way."

They were walking down a narrow hallway that was mostly a bottleneck between two larger sections of the upstairs area. Just as he stepped into the hall, Clint saw another woman enter it from the opposite end.

All the other women might have carried themselves as if they were goddesses, but this one hardly seemed to act at all. Her beauty surrounded her like an aura and all it took was a subtle smile for her to make Clint want to forget everything else he might have been doing.

She wore a dress made of lace that was the color of fresh peaches. The bodice was cut low and revealed a figure that was beyond impressive. Large, rounded breasts swayed gently as she walked, as did the thick, golden brown curls of her hair.

"Excuse me," she said softly as she walked by.

The gunman leading the way practically ignored her, but Clint wasn't able to pull off that trick. He put his back to the wall so she could get by, but that didn't stop her from brushing against him as she walked. The touch of her body against him was full of warm promise and the scent of her perfume was just strong enough to make its presence known.

She paused for a moment before moving on, studying Clint with quick passes from her sharp eyes. After she'd gotten a look at him, the sultry smile that had been on her face was replaced by another type of expression. The shift was so obvious, that it brought Clint up short.

There was an urgency about her which hadn't been there before. It showed through for a brief flicker of time. It showed up even more when she whispered, "My name is Estrella. Come find me when you can."

Before Clint could respond, he felt a grip around his arm as he was pulled along by the gunman.

"Come on," the gunman grunted. "You can fuck whoever you want when Mr. Gilliam's through with you."

Clint pulled his arm out of the other man's grip and locked eyes with him in a razor-edged glare. Normally, he wouldn't have appreciated being talked to in such a way, but the gunman's words seemed particularly inappropriate considering their surroundings.

"Apologize to the lady," Clint said.

The gunman scoffed and started to walk in the same direction he'd been going before. This time, it was Clint who stopped their progress as he took hold of the gunman just long enough to shove him against the closest wall.

"Why should I apologize to some whore?" the gunman asked.

Moving his hand just close enough to the Colt at his side to bring it to the other man's notice, Clint said, "Because I'm asking you real nicely."

After a moment's consideration, the gunman rolled his eyes, looked over to Estrella and said, "Sorry about that."

"That's better," Clint said. "Lead on."

The gunman muttered something under his breath, but none of it could be heard over the stomping of his boots against the floor. As soon as he cleared the hall, his stomping grew even louder until he was practically knocking flower vases off their tables from five paces away.

Estrella was at the other end of the hall by now and watching everything that was taking place. Her full, light-red lips curled into an amused smile as the gunman continued to pitch his walking fit.

Tipping his hat, Clint noticed a troubled look in the woman's eyes which had eased a bit, but still remained after the gunman was put into his place. "I'll see you in a bit, Estrella."

"I hope so, Mr. Adams." With that, she turned and walked away.

Finding Estrella had been a pleasant surprise. The fact that she knew his name was a surprise as well. Clint figured he'd find out soon enough just how pleasant that surprise actually was.

NINETEEN

The staircase leading up to the third floor was all but hidden in one of the rooms separate from the second floor lounge. Unlike most of the other rooms on that floor, this one wasn't a bedroom. It was Kathy's office and the stairs in the back looked as if they led up to an attic.

Once Clint followed his armed escort up those stairs, he saw that the third floor was a whole lot more than just another attic. While it might have been that much at one time, it was now fitted with all the comforts of a normal office and even put Kathy's to shame. Of course, compared to Bradshaw's office, it was still an attic.

The silver-haired man who'd invited Clint inside now sat behind a desk and motioned toward the chairs in front of him. "Please, come in," he said graciously. "What do you think of my little place of business?"

Clint took one more look around, shrugged and said, "I've seen better."

The man behind the desk smiled, but it looked more like a predator showing its teeth. "If I hadn't known that you'd already paid Mr. Bradshaw a visit, I might have taken offense to that. Then again, after the way you were received outside, I can see why you'd still be a little bent out of shape. Hopefully I can rectify that."

"Bent out of shape?" Clint asked. "I guess you could say that. Especially since one of your boys over there nearly bent my entire face out of shape using his fists."

"You're a tough man, Mr. Adams. I'm sure you'll be just fine."

Clint nodded. "I see you already know who I am."

"You're not an easy man to miss."

"And I suppose you're Mr. Gilliam."

"I'm not an easy man to miss, either. Not in this town, anyway."

"I was on my way to have a word with you before I was sidetracked."

"Then by all means, have your word. Can I interest you in that drink?"

Clint shook his head.

Snapping his fingers, Gilliam had to wait all of five seconds before a large, bulbous glass was set on his desk by a woman who'd been keeping so far in the background that Clint hadn't even noticed her. She was a slender Chinese woman with silken black hair flowing freely over her shoulders. After she'd filled Gilliam's glass, the woman flinched when he reached out to take hold of it.

"Just breaking in a new worker," Gilliam said while nodding toward the young woman. "Once they're good at serving me, serving our customers is a simple matter. You certain I can't have her get something for you?"

Now that he knew she was there, Clint took a moment to study the young woman a bit closer. The way she carried herself and averted her eyes spoke volumes. She was afraid of every man in the room, but feared Gilliam the most.

Her pale skin was almost flawless. At least, it seemed that way until Clint got a look at part of her that was exposed once the neckline of her filmy dress slipped to one side. The shift of material didn't expose anything more than the lower slope of her neck, but it also allowed part of a dark bruise to slip into view.

Looking even closer for a moment, Clint managed to see bruises peeking from her loose sleeves as well as a few small round scars that were more than likely burns from a cigar being put out on her flesh. Suddenly, the Chinese woman became aware of what Clint was seeing and she pulled her clothing over the wounds. Her eyes darted away and she quickly found a shadow in which to hide.

"Once again, I apologize for you being wrapped up in that nasty business outside," Gilliam said. "That wretch of a man you were standing near owes me a considerable amount of money."

"Actually, that's exactly what I wanted to talk to you about."

Once that had been said, the air within Gilliam's office stopped moving. Everything stopped moving, in fact, leaving only the occasional nervous glance to keep the place from looking like a painting.

Noises from the floors below found their way through the wooden barriers. Even the wind seemed to push especially hard against the large round window on the other side of the room.

"Is this about the offer you made to my associate?" Gilliam asked.

"Pretty much."

"And why would you want to do such a thing? Is Mr. Johanssen a friend of yours?"

"Let's just say that Mr. Johanssen doesn't deserve to be pushed around the way he has been."

"And how would you know that?"

"Because," Clint replied in a steely voice, "nobody deserves to be pushed around like that."

"I'm a businessman, Mr. Adams. Nothing more."

"Great. Then you can transfer Mr. Johanssen's debt to me and it'll be taken care of in a very businesslike manner."

Gilliam leaned back and steepled his fingers in front of him. He then started tapping the ends of his fingers against his chin while slowly taking in the sight before him. While he'd seemed annoyed at first, he now seemed more perplexed than anything else.

"There's other matters going on here, Mr. Adams. I've got other deals in the works and other things to consider besides just Mr. Johanssen's debt."

All this time, Gilliam hadn't been the only one studying the situation. Clint's eyes and ears were wide open as well and he was learning a hell of a lot just by sitting calmly in his seat.

One of those things he noticed was the way the Chinese girl flinched when Gilliam mentioned the other deals he had in the works.

"How long has Wilbur been paying off this debt?" Clint asked.

"Not long enough."

"Will it ever be long enough?"

Clint's question hung in the air, loaded with meaning. Not one of those meanings went unnoticed by Gilliam. In fact, he seemed to read enough between Clint's lines that he was starting to look at Clint in an entirely different way.

"I've heard plenty about you, Mr. Adams," Gilliam said. "One of those things was that you don't keep your nose out of other people's business."

"Sometimes that's the way it's got to be," Clint replied.

"Otherwise, there would be a whole lot of bad business going on."

"Well, I'm not just some asshole who stays behind his desk," Gilliam said as his voice grew into a loud rumble. Pushing himself back, Gilliam caused his chair to clatter against the floor until he was able to stand up with both hands planted firmly on the top of his desk. Leaning forward, Gilliam started to resemble a large buzzard squaring off over a disputed corpse. His hooked nose turned red as his nostrils flared. When he spoke, he pounded his desk for emphasis.

"I have been polite, Mr. Adams," Gilliam fumed. "And you look at me like I'm some kind of small-timer who should be afraid of you. I conduct my business as I see fit, and I cannot be seen as someone who allows themselves to be used by the likes of Wilbur Johanssen!

"Neither can I allow any of my loans to go unpaid. There are consequences for crossing me and, by God, you or that shit-for-brains Johanssen have seen the half of what those consequences entail. This is about free trade, Mr. Adams! That's something this country was founded on."

Clint remained in his seat and refused to let himself get riled up by the words that were being shouted at him. Instead, he kept his eyes locked on Gilliam and spoke in a tone that was calm, but sharp enough to cut through all the steam filling the air.

"I didn't come up here to tell you how to run your business," Clint said. "I came up here to talk about a robbery committed by one of your men."

"Robbery? What the hell are you talking about?"

"One of your men beat the tar out of Wilbur and tore his wedding ring right off his finger. Is that how you want to be seen by everyone in town?"

Gilliam took in a few rasping breaths and started glancing about the room. When his eyes settled upon a man lounging near the window, he asked, "Is that true, O'Shea?"

O'Shea nodded.

"You still have this ring he's talking about?"

Grudgingly, the gunman dug in his pocket to remove something which he tossed through the air toward Gilliam's desk.

Gilliam snatched the thing from the air and turned it over in his hand. The ring glinted weakly as light bounced off of dented gold. "Here," he said, pitching it toward Clint. "Take it. But tell Mr. Johanssen to keep his payments coming or I'll step up the interest."

Clint pocketed the ring, stood up and nodded. "Here," he said, digging into his pockets until he found the money he was after. "This should square him up for a little while."

Gilliam looked down at the money Clint offered as though he didn't know what he was seeing. Finally, he took the cash and dropped it into one of his desk's drawers. "You're a reasonable man after all, Mr. Adams," he said in a voice that was caught somewhere between a rasp and a snarl. "Glad to do business with you. I'm sure you can see your own way out."

"More than happy to," Clint said as he got up and tipped his hat to Gilliam. He took another look around him as well, acknowledging each gunman in turn.

Jack still looked as if he meant to tear Clint's throat out, but kept himself in check for the time being.

O'Shea still stood with his arms at his sides. Judging by that stance, he either expected to have Wilbur's ring tossed back to him or to draw his gun and fire. When neither happened, he wound up just glaring angrily at Clint.

Once he was outside of the office and walking back down to the second floor lounge, Clint let out the breath that had been building up inside of him. He looked down at the ring he was holding and could pick out flecks of dried blood crusted onto the inside of the band.

His face was still aching and his knuckles still reminded him of the punches he'd delivered. Sometimes, doing a good deed was a whole lot of trouble.

TWENTY

Clint took his time walking through the second floor lounge. There was no shortage of pretty faces and attractive figures to catch his eye, but there was one face in particular that he was looking for. When he reached the top of the stairs before spotting that face, Clint stepped up to the closest woman who wasn't already talking to someone else.

"Well, hello there," the shapely blonde said as she sidled up next to Clint. "You look like you need some company."

"Actually, I was looking for Estrella. Do you know where she is?"

The blonde nodded. Her smile grew even wider. "Oh, so you're the one she was waiting for? Her room's right down the hall and the second on the left. Just knock before you walk in. Wouldn't want to catch her before she was ready for you."

Her words and tone of voice made Clint feel as though he was in for more than a conversation. Then again, he was certain that that had been her intent the entire time.

Clint found the door she'd pointed him toward without a problem and knocked on it a few times. Before he opened it, he remembered what went on in most of those rooms and waited for her to open it instead.

The door came open just a bit at first, allowing a single eye to peer through the opening. As soon as she saw who was outside, Estrella opened the door the rest of the way and reached out to grab hold of Clint's hand.

"It's you," she said in an excited whisper. "I'm so glad you came."

Clint allowed himself to be pulled into the room so she could shut and lock the door behind him. "Do I know you?" he asked.

"I doubt it. We only met in passing a few months ago in Nevada. Actually, we weren't even introduced."

"Then, I hate to be rude, but—"

"I know who you are and I saw what you did to help a man who was put into a jail where he didn't belong. His name was—"

Snapping his fingers, Clint stepped in and interrupted this time. "Joe Maven. He was accused of killing his cousin with an axe handle."

She smiled and nodded. "He was going to hang for it, too, until you came along to clear it up."

"It wasn't too difficult to see that something was off about that matter. I think the fact that he was still wearing his good arm in a sling gave away the fact that he couldn't exactly club anyone to death. That, added to the way he limped made the story of him running from the body even more preposterous."

"You saved that man's life."

"I just asked the right questions and followed them up."

"But nobody else would have done that," Estrella said. "Most folks just like to see things get wrapped up and put away. They don't care about who gets hurt along the way."

"So what does any of this have to do with you?"

"I'm in a similar situation, Mr. Adams." Suddenly, Estrella stopped what she was saying and leaned in close to the door. Heavy footsteps came from the hallway and she didn't relax again until they'd passed. "I'm stuck here just like that man was stuck in that Nevada jail cell."

"What do you mean?"

"I'm paying off a debt and I realized that no matter how much I do or earn, it'll never get paid off. Not until I'm dead."

"Who do you owe this debt to?"

Her eyes lowered and she took a moment to gather up her courage. Even before she got herself to speak the name out loud, Clint knew what he was going to hear.

"Mr. Gilliam," Estrella told him. "I wanted to get out and see the West and he paid for my ticket from Georgia. Since then, I needed clothes, food and a place to live. He gave me a loan for all of that and I've been paying on it ever since.

"When I hit a rough patch and couldn't pay for a month or two, he said I could work for him here." She'd just started to lift her face to look at Clint directly, but that quickly changed and she averted her eyes. "It started out with me serving drinks, but then he wanted me to work . . . upstairs. I said no, but he said I could either take my chances with these men or share my bed with him and his men.

"I've seen other girls who shared Mr. Gilliam's bed. They come away from that looking like they were trampled by a horse. Some of them don't even come out at all."

Estrella's predicament wasn't entirely unheard of. Plenty of pimps and slavers got people to work for them as a way to work off a debt or earn their way to someplace supposedly better than where they'd started out. Some of those girls knew what they were getting in to. Plenty more of them didn't have the faintest idea.

That is, they didn't know until it was too late to do anything about it.

"How long have you been paying off this debt?" Clint asked.

"Three years. What I borrowed should have been repaid three times over by now."

"Why didn't you ever just leave? You seem like a strong and smart enough woman for that."

"Up until now, I've been trying to do my part and not get hurt. Lately, Mr. Gilliam says I'm getting restless and has been keeping watch on me. He's even . . . hurt other girls as an example. He says that bruising me up would only cut into his profits."

Clint reached out and put his hands on her shoulders. Estrella felt soft and warm in his embrace and began moving closer to him on her own accord. Before she could get too close, however, she was gently shifted to look at the back of the room.

"You've got a window right there," Clint said. "Use it."

"I can't just leave. Mr. Gilliam will find me. Whether it's him or one of his men they'll both—"

"Use that window just after dark tonight," Clint interrupted.

"Why tonight?"

"Because that's when I'll be waiting to catch you."

TWENTY-ONE

When Clint got back to his hotel, there was no message waiting for him. Although it would have been good to know that Wilbur had collected his wife and some things to stay somewhere else, it had been less than an hour since he'd last seen the other man.

Clint walked back to his room and sat down at the small round table across from his bed. Removing the Colt from its holster, he began taking the gun apart and setting each piece upon the table so it could be cleaned. Although he didn't get to practice his craft as often as he would have liked, Clint was still a gunsmith and going through the old motions felt like slipping on a familiar pair of boots.

Doing so gave him a chance to sit and think about what had happened in the past day. Anyone else might have been overwhelmed by it all, but Clint's life was a far cry from anything ordinary. Just when he thought he might get to spend some uneventful time in Los Tejanos, it turned out that Bradshaw's simple request had opened a whole other mess entirely.

Like the pieces of Clint's Colt, the events that he'd seen weren't much when set out all by themselves. The Colt broke down to a cylinder, a hammer, a barrel and several other components that weren't much more than simple shapes made from iron.

His stay in Los Tejanos broke down into a selfish offer, a man found beaten and robbed in the street, a fistfight and a woman being forced to stay in a brothel. When put together, however, those things all formed a single picture.

At the middle of that picture, one way or another, was Boyle Gilliam.

Although Clint doubted that Bradshaw had much to do with Gilliam, it was a certainty that he had worked with the man who made his office in Rosie's attic. After all, it had been Bradshaw who'd known all too well where to find Gilliam.

Wilbur Johanssen was getting steered by Gilliam like a donkey getting pulled by the bit in its mouth. Clint had seen it too many times: gamblers thinking they're going to make their big win being preyed upon by men who saw such hopes as a business opportunity.

Even if the men who loaned out that kind of money didn't get it back right away, they oftentimes got it trickled back to them for the rest of the borrower's life. Once enough of those trickles were combined, it formed a stream that was enough to account for some healthy profits. Actually, it was a pretty smart scheme. All that was required was a chunk of money to loan out and the lack of morals to bleed people dry like a leach attached to their necks for the rest of their lives.

Odds were real good that Gilliam wasn't even marking off any of the cash he'd gotten in return from Wilbur. All of it was chalked up to interest. Clint had seen proof of that already. Since O'Shea hadn't even handed over the ring he'd stolen, it was obvious that Wilbur's debt would never be considered repaid.

And that brought Clint to Estrella. He was somewhat weary of taking her story at face value, but that was only because she'd come from out of nowhere to tell it to him.

Clint's first instinct was to wonder what she was after. If he hadn't seen that Chinese girl being treated like a slave in Gilliam's office, Clint might not have believed much of Estrella's story at all.

But he had seen her. The terror and shame in that Chinese girl's face was enough to make Clint wince. He'd also seen enough to know that Gilliam would be capable of doing something like putting that look into the poor girl's eyes.

The Chinese girl was young, pretty and should have been full of life. Instead, she looked as if she'd already filled her few years on this earth with misery and pain. She had the look of a whipped dog and that was a damn terrible thing to see in anyone's eyes.

The more he thought about all of this, the more Clint's hands worked at cleaning the pieces of the Colt. It was to the point now where he wasn't just wiping away the dust, powder and grit from all the moving parts. He was tearing into them with the force he'd been holding back when he'd been face-to-face with Gilliam and his men.

It would have been so easy to draw that gun and go to work outside of Rosie's. Just wiping that smug look off of Jack's face would have been worth the effort. Seeing how quick they were to throw a punch or start shoving folks around, Clint was certain that anything he would have done to them would have been justified.

But that wasn't the way good men conducted themselves.

That was the way vigilantes conducted themselves and it was a real short ride from being a vigilante to becoming someone who needed to be hunted down themselves. That was the type of decision that weighed the heaviest on him every time Clint's hand drifted toward his holster.

Pulling the trigger too quickly one time or waiting to do so for too long could spell disaster. Then again, putting his gun away for good was no longer an option, either. It would only be a matter of time before someone came along who wanted to count the death of The Gunsmith among their short list of accomplishments.

Those kinds of killers didn't much care whether or not a man was armed. Shooting a famous gunman in the back was just as good as outdrawing him. Whoever was left standing could just make up whatever story they wanted.

Shaking his head at the sad truth of it all, Clint eased up on the piece he was cleaning and took a moment to look at the bits of iron strewn out before him like some kind of puzzle. Most of them were shining by this point and already laid out in the relative position they needed to be. In fact, the disassembly was so perfect that it looked as though the Colt had just been pulled apart an inch or so in every possible direction.

The sight seemed so clean and so perfect. There was no guesswork involved when taking a gun apart and putting it back together. No black or white and no dire consequences for trying something different.

That was the appeal of Clint's craft and the reason that he would never let himself stray too far from his roots. Just looking at the pieces and knowing that he could fit them all together slowed his pulse and made him take calmer breaths.

The whole world could go to hell, but that Colt would always come apart and fit together again in the same exact way.

It turned out that his sense of calm came at just the right time.

Once his thoughts had quieted down and he was focusing on nothing but the table in front of him, Clint heard a hushed voice coming through the wall directly in front of him. Actually, it was a couple of hushed voices followed by the slow shuffle of boots making their way down the hall toward his door.

". . . sure he's in there?" one of the voices said.

"Yeah. We'll find . . . soon enough."

Clint's ears perked up at the sound of that and his hands froze over the scattered pieces of his Colt. Even his heart seemed to stop before taking its next beat as he listened for any trace of the next sound coming from outside his door.

There were a few more footsteps, taken slowly and deliberately. There was also a single click that was unmistakable to any gunsmith's ears. That click was a hammer being cocked into position and it was too deep to belong to anything but a shotgun.

The footsteps stopped right outside his door, casting a set of shadows beneath it and into Clint's room.

TWENTY-TWO

Even before he saw the shadows being cast from the other side of his door, Clint was taking action. Since his rifle was laying on the other side of the room next to his saddlebags, he knew he couldn't get to it before that shotgunner got to him.

Although he wasn't much for carrying more than one gun at a time, there did happen to be a smaller pistol in Clint's room. Unfortunately, that was in his saddlebags, which meant it was no help to him whatsoever.

That left his weapon of choice, which was the Colt that was in several pieces on the table in front of him.

All of this flew through Clint's mind in the blink of an eye. Before that blink was over, his hands were already flying into motion to pick up the Colt's pieces and fit them together again. Outside his door, there were at least two men standing in the hall preparing themselves to come inside.

They bickered quietly to see who would go through first, which gave Clint an extra second or two to do a job that had suddenly taken on life-and-death consequences.

Putting the pieces back together too slowly would leave Clint unarmed to the men who were already trying to open the door by pulling on the handle.

Putting the gun together again too quickly might make it seize up or backfire when the trigger was pulled. Either way, that would make the only remaining question whether Clint would get hit by his own bullet or a bullet from someone else.

The door rattled on its hinges as the men outside found out for themselves that it was locked. All the while, Clint's hands flew to put the gun together while his eyes darted back and forth between his current task and the door leading to the hallway.

By the time the men had given up on trying to open the door the easy way, Clint was fitting the barrel and cylinder into place. Most of the actions that brought the Colt together were so engrained in Clint's mind that he barely even realized he was doing them.

All he focused on was following the familiar chain of movements while trying to do them fast enough to save his life.

As Clint was reaching the final stages of getting the Colt ready to fire, a boot slammed against his door to buckle it within its frame. The door held against that first kick, buying Clint a precious fraction of a second. It didn't hold up against the second kick, however, and came slamming inward to let the men charge into Clint's room with their weapons at the ready.

The sound of Clint fitting the last piece into place was overpowered by the sound of the door hitting the wall. Two men rushed into Clint's room; both of their faces were covered by bandannas. By the time those men had spotted the table where Clint was sitting, the modified Colt was put together and pointed directly at them.

Acting on pure reflex, Clint aimed the gun as soon as he got it in his hand. He squeezed the trigger, even though one thing was nagging at the back of his mind.

The hammer reached back and snapped forward, landing squarely on an empty chamber.

The Colt was in one piece again, but that piece didn't include any ammunition.

For a moment, all three men looked at each other across the room. Clint was trying desperately to think of what to do next while the other two were waiting to feel hot lead rip through their bodies. When the shot didn't come, the masked men let out the breath they'd been holding and quickly reminded themselves of why they'd busted into the room in the first place.

As the intruders' guns were swinging around to aim at Clint, they were already having to duck for cover themselves.

Since he'd already known the gun would be empty a split second before firing it, Clint was plotting out his next move. Everything was happening so quickly that he didn't get more than a half second to think, but that was all he needed.

Clint knew there were spare bullets on his gun belt. All he needed was a few moments to get them into the Colt. To buy himself those extra moments, Clint tipped his chair back until he felt himself start to tip over toward the floor. Rather than try to readjust his balance, he let himself fall back while straightening both legs.

As he went over, Clint felt both feet connect with the bottom of the table in front of him. His own momentum was more than enough to knock the table onto its side and fall toward the incoming intruders. Clint's back hit the floor at about the same time as the table did, both impacts filling the room with chaotic noise.

Once he and the table were both down, Clint turned to press his cheek against the floor and pull his legs down as well. Just as he'd expected, the shotgun roared and filled the room with smoke and hot lead. Chunks of the table disappeared amid a spray of splinters and buckshot hissed over the spot where Clint was laying.

Although the table wasn't very big, it was large enough

to block the gunmen's view as well as catch that first shot. When he opened his eyes, Clint realized that the table wouldn't be good for much more than that since it had nearly been blown in half already.

"Get around on that side," one of the men said in a voice muffled by the bandanna covering his face. "I'll take this one."

Clint wasn't able to see which man was going in which direction, but that didn't really matter much anyhow. All he needed to know was that they were on their way. His only concern was to be ready for them.

Of course, since he needed to be off his back and holding a loaded gun, being ready wasn't exactly as easy as it sounded.

TWENTY-THREE

Both of the masked men knew who they were dealing with. That fact alone made them take their time when working their way around the table Clint had knocked over. While the guns in their hands gave them some backbone, it wasn't enough for them to go charging forward now that The Gunsmith himself knew he was in their sights.

Using a combination of glances and hand signals, the intruders moved around the table while keeping themselves low. At the last moment, one of them jumped around the table while the other straightened up to get a look at what Clint was doing.

Neither one of them could see the slightest trace of Clint, who'd pressed himself against what was left of the table rather than take one of the more obvious escape routes.

He announced his own presence by the metallic snap of the Colt's cylinder being closed. By the time the shotgunner shifted his eyes to find Clint pressed against the remains of the table, it was too late for him to do much about it.

Even so, Clint allowed the man one second to do the right thing. Instead, the masked man began turning the shotgun toward him while desperation filled his eyes.

Using his right leg against the back of one of the table's legs, Clint sent the table into the masked man's shins. The painful impact was just enough to get the man to buckle a bit, which caused the shotgun to point toward the floor rather than at Clint's chest.

Surprisingly enough, the shotgunner kept himself from pulling the trigger. Before he could readjust his aim, he was knocked back a step by a shot from the modified Colt. The bullet tore a path through his ribs and was quickly followed by another round which punched straight through his heart.

The intruder closest to Clint was dead before he hit the floor. The shotgun he'd been holding didn't even hit the floor, since it was caught by a quickly outstretched hand.

As soon as he'd grabbed the shotgun, Clint rolled toward the body that had just dropped onto the floor. The moment he cleared the spot where he'd been hiding, Clint heard a quick series of shots that punched through the floor, the wall behind him as well as the remains of the table.

Although he didn't use shotguns all that often, Clint didn't need to know much to be able to point the hefty gun over his shoulder and squeeze the trigger to cover himself as he looked for some better cover.

The shotgun blasted in his ear, sending its smoky cargo behind him while nearly deafening him in the process. Clint's ears rang horribly as every other sound in the world was blotted out. When he moved, he couldn't hear his own footsteps. He couldn't even hear what the second intruder was doing.

All Clint could hear just then was the piercing shriek left behind from the shotgun's blast and the thumping of his own heart slamming against his ribs.

There wasn't much else inside the room except for the bed and a washbasin. Since he seemed to have bought himself a little more time than he'd expected, Clint stopped moving and picked a spot to stand his ground.

That spot was directly beside the bed and a few feet from the window looking down onto the main street outside his hotel. Knowing the shotgun was empty, Clint let it drop from his hand as he squared his shoulders and faced down the remaining intruder.

TWENTY-FOUR

One of the benefits of a shotgun was the fact that nearly anyone could hit their target if they were closer than ten feet to it. In the confines of the hotel room, Clint would have had a more difficult time missing the other man than hitting him. That became painfully obvious when he saw the blood soaking into the intruder's shirt from a fresh wound in his side.

Actually, a good portion of one arm had been blown off. Clint would have felt a lot more comfortable if the intruder's gun arm was the one to take the damage.

Although Clint often wondered how long it would take for him to go deaf from all the gunshots he'd heard, this was not the day for it to happen. Instead, the ringing in his ears cleared up as the gritty black fog of smoke cleared up from the air around him.

The intruder stayed on his feet, but it seemed to be nothing more than luck that kept him from toppling over. Blood streamed down from the fresh wound to pool around his boots. The gun in his hand was all but forgotten.

"Take that mask off," Clint ordered.

But the intruder could only blink a few times and sway as the pain started to sink in.

Clint kept his pistol trained on the other man as he stepped forward and swatted the gun from the intruder's hand. It fell and clattered to the floor where Clint was able to kick it away. From there, Clint reached out and pulled the bandanna off of the man's face.

Taking a moment to study the intruder, Clint wasn't able to find anything about him that seemed familiar.

"Who sent you?" Clint asked.

There was somewhat of a glimmer returning to the intruder's eyes, but he was a long way from being fully conscious of his surroundings.

Clint stepped in front of the man so he was the only thing the intruder could see. "Who sent you?" he repeated. "Was it Gilliam?"

Although that name got a reaction from the intruder, it wasn't much more than a twitching shift of his eyes.

Clint had played plenty of poker in his lifetime for that twitch to be more than enough to suit his purposes.

"What did Gilliam want? Why'd he send someone to shoot me?"

Just then, the man lost all the color in his face and he started wobbling on his feet. Before Clint could do anything about it, the intruder had teetered off balance and then dropped onto the floor. He landed awkwardly on his backside and shook his head as if he'd been smacked with a shovel.

"You're about to pass out from losing all that blood," Clint said. "Stay put and I'll see about getting a doctor."

While Clint was certain plenty of people in the hotel had to have heard the shooting, he knew it would take some convincing to get one of those people to come out from wherever they were hiding. He stepped around the intruder and headed for the door, which now hung dangling from a single hinge.

He wasn't about to let the man from his sight, however, which was something that wound up saving Clint's life.

Just as he was about to step into the hall, Clint saw the intruder start to move. At first, it looked as though he was just going to fall over the rest of the way, but then it was clear that he was reaching for the pistol he'd dropped moments ago.

After gathering up all of the strength he could, the intruder sucked in a breath and lunged for his pistol. His fingers closed around the grip as he shifted around to point the barrel at Clint. Although he was falling over as he moved, he still managed to get Clint in his sights.

Clint didn't want to shoot the wounded man, but his only other choice was to let that same man take a shot at him. Aiming from the hip, Clint aimed and squeezed off a shot in a fraction of a second. The Colt barked once more to send a round into the intruder's forehead and out the other side of his skull.

The gun in the man's hand went off as his finger pulled the trigger with his final, twitching reflex. It sent a shot into the floor only a foot and a half short of its target before it slid out from between dead fingers.

Clint didn't flinch when the bullet tore up a chunk of floor next to his boot. "Dammit," he said under his breath.

Now that both men were dead, there wasn't a whole lot they could tell him. Just to cover all angles, he figured he might as well check through their pockets to see if he might get a clue from there. As it turned out, all Clint needed to do was take off the shotgunner's mask to get the answer he needed.

"Gotcha," Clint whispered as he looked down upon the familiar face. Jack was pale and lifeless, but he still wore the bruises that Clint had given him earlier. And unless he'd started hiring himself out to someone else in the last couple of hours, he still worked for Mr. Boyle Gilliam.

TWENTY-FIVE

"You all right, Mr. Adams?" The owner of the hotel where Clint was staying might have been a bit late, but he showed some guts in showing up at all. That went double when he stuck around even after getting a look at the two dead bodies stacked inside of one of his rooms.

Clint had draped sheets over the two dead men and was on his way out when he'd almost run over the owner. A skinny, middle-aged man with thinning brown hair and beady eyes, the owner couldn't get himself to move fast enough to get out of Clint's way. That resulted in both men colliding just outside of Clint's door.

"Has anyone gone for the sheriff yet?" Clint asked.

"I thought I'd check and see what was going on before involving him. Saves me some money that way."

"Saves you money?"

The owner nodded. "We can't just bring the sheriff in on every little thing. He charges us for any time of his that gets wasted."

"Oh, I see. How about I go find him myself?"

"Be my guest," the owner said while stepping aside. "He tends to hurry more for strangers anyway."

Rather than waste time trying to get that explained to

104

him, Clint rushed out of the hotel and hurried down the street toward the sheriff's office. Although he'd been in town a little while, he hadn't seen much of the law since he introduced himself to a deputy after arriving. The deputy had been more concerned with impressing a barmaid and hadn't given Clint more than a wave to brush him off. Clint felt fortunate to get the location of the sheriff's office from the kid.

Once he pointed himself in the right direction, Clint only had to walk to the next corner before he was the one that was almost run down by a big man in a hurry. This man wore a hat the size of Texas and had enough whiskers sprouting from his face to cover him in a dark, graying mask.

"Step aside, son! Didn't you hear the shots?" the man in the big hat snorted.

Apart from the hat and whiskers, something else caught Clint's eye regarding the other man. Mostly, that was the badge pinned to his lapel.

"I was just coming to see you about that very thing," Clint replied.

The big man stopped. When he did so, his thumbs found their way to his gun belt and hooked in behind the leather strap which was buckled loosely around an ample midsection. "Is that a fact? I heard the shots came from the Comfort Arms. Are you a guest there?"

"Yes, and I am also the one they shot at."

Sometimes, all Clint needed to see was how someone reacted to something. When the sheriff heard that little bit of news, he barely batted an eye. In fact, going on the look on his face alone, he might have just heard someone tell him that water was wet.

"Well," the lawman said. "That's a damn shame. At least it don't look like you got yourself hurt."

"No," Clint said, already writing the man off in his mind. "I'm doing just fine. Just check my room for a couple of Gilliam's men. They're not doing so well."

With that, Clint started to walk away. That was all he needed to do to get a reaction from the lawman. Although the man was thick around the middle, he did a good job of catching up to Clint before he managed to get too far away from him.

"Hold on there, stranger. Maybe you ought to tell me a little more."

When the sheriff got ahold of Clint's arm, he held on with a firm enough grip to let him know he wasn't about to get away. "Come on back with me and show me what happened."

After shaking free of the lawman's grasp, Clint brought him all the way back to his room. By the time they got back, there was a good-sized crowd gathering outside of the Comfort Arms. The crowd leaked into the hotel itself and up the stairs leading to Clint's room.

All along the way, the sheriff worked his way through the crowd. All he really needed to do was make his presence known and most everyone stepped aside from him. He and Clint were almost to the room with the busted door when the owner of the hotel spotted the lawman and came running toward him.

"Sheriff Donner, I'm so glad you came. I was just about to send for you."

"Yeah," Clint said. "I just hope this isn't too expensive of a trip."

Hearing that, the lawman wheeled around to get another look at Clint. "Now, I see what's stuck in your craw. That doesn't sound too good when it's put that way, does it?"

"No sir," Clint replied. "It doesn't."

"Well, I'm one of the men that started up this town with Mark Bradshaw. Sometimes people think the law is just there to make house calls like we're some kind of doctors. Well, my time is money and if too much time gets wasted with breaking up fights and pulling apart quarrelling wives and husbands, then I charge 'em for it. It's either that or raise the taxes for everyone. I see this as a whole lot more fair."

Clint could tell that Sheriff Donner thought he was describing some kind of perfect system. Oddly enough, the looks on the faces of everyone else around made it seem as though they went right along with him.

Shrugging, Clint said, "Whatever works for you, Sheriff. I just thought you'd like to see what's left to see before you came around looking to drag me in."

"Yer a smart man, Adams. I see Mark really knew what he was talking about when he suggested you for that plan of mine."

"So that was your plan he was talking about?"

"Yep."

"That explains a bit."

Putting on his stern, official face, Sheriff Donner hooked his thumbs through his gun belt and walked up to get a closer look at the door. It was still hanging by one hinge.

The hotel owner stayed right behind the lawman, fretting nervously. "I heard the shots and came running. Near as I could tell—"

"Adams told me the whole story," Donner interrupted. The sheriff kept walking into the room and then took a gander at the pair of bodies laying there as though he was inspecting another piece of broken furniture. All the while, he nodded and grumbled to himself. Finally, he straightened up and beamed as though he'd just had an epiphany.

"Looks like Adams's story checks out," Donner announced. "Let's hear yours now."

Seeing that he was the one in Donner's sights, the hotel owner gave his account of what happened. His story boiled down to when he'd heard what and ended with him doing his best to make sure he wasn't wasting the sheriff's valuable time.

"Seems like all the ducks are in a row," Sheriff Donner

said. "I'll make sure the undertaker comes by to collect these here bodies."

Clint had spent enough time dealing with lawmen to know that seeking them out when something like this happened was a good idea. If anything, it saved a whole lot of trouble when they came to find him and it didn't hurt to make it known that he had nothing to hide. But, after seeing Sheriff Donner in action, Clint felt like he should charge the lawman for wasting his time.

"Is that all?" Clint asked.

Donner looked like he was expecting a slap on the back. "Well, yeah. For now, anyway."

"I guess I'll be finding somewhere else to stay."

Before Clint left, he heard Donner make one more announcement. "Oh, and there won't be any charge for this little visit."

TWENTY-SIX

Clint had long ago realized there were three types of lawmen. There were honest, hardworking ones. There were crooked ones who were actually good at their jobs, and there were ones that were just plain useless. Donner fell so solidly into the third category that the Texan's ass made a thump when it hit the bottom.

At least now he could see how the problems in Los Tejanos had become so bad for certain people. Of course, that understanding didn't really help matters very much. If it wasn't for the fact that there were some folks who really needed someone to lend them a hand, Clint would have put the town behind him and not looked back.

The day was dragging on and Clint spent a good portion of it nursing a glass of lemonade outside of Greely's General Store. The shop was located on one of the busiest streets in town, which allowed Clint to sit in the shade and watch folks wander past him.

There were a few folks that interested him a little more than the rest, however. For the most part, those folks were stomping in and out of Rosie's Gentlemen's Club which was just down the street from the spot Clint had chosen. In fact, Greely's General Store was positioned perfectly for

Clint to watch the club while being partially hidden by the passing crowd.

As the hours slipped by, several people came and went from Rosie's. They were men for the most part and they usually left with a much bigger smile than the one they'd worn on their way in. The ones that weren't smiling were the ones wearing their guns and strutting like peacocks.

Those were Gilliam's boys. If Clint couldn't spot them by the iron at their sides, the glare etched onto their faces was more than enough to clear up the confusion.

Clint wasn't alone on the porch of the general store. There were plenty of fellows who passed the time along with him, shooting the breeze and tipping their hats to the ladies. Some of those men came and went and some of them even found their way into Rosie's before too long so they could come back to the porch and brag about it.

If it wasn't for those fellas on the porch who quickly brought Clint into their routine of swapping bad jokes and telling tall tales, the day would have gone by a whole lot slower. On a more practical note, the gunmen walking in and out of Rosie's would have spotted him a whole lot quicker as well.

It wasn't until early evening that some of the gunmen started to pause before stepping through Rosie's door. The first one to notice Clint at all was the gunman who'd played second fiddle when Jack had tried to knock Wilbur around outside of the club earlier that day. At the time, Clint was fairly certain that the quieter of the two gunmen was the one in charge.

Now, he was sure of it.

The gunman stopped just before walking into the gentleman's club and took a long look down the street.

"Uh oh," mumbled one of the old men sitting on the porch along with Clint. "Looks like the troublemaker's taking an interest in us."

"You think so, Larry?" Clint asked, having picked up all of the other men's names throughout the day.

Larry was a slender fellow who looked tougher than most of the younger men carrying supplies out of the general store. His head was covered with a thick layer of white hair and his voice was the one heard the most when it came to the group's jokes and stories.

"Oh yeah," Larry said. "Ol' Mace don't need to look at much of anything for more than a second or two. When he stops like that, there's usually trouble." Turning to look at Clint, he added, "I'd say you're the one in his sights, partner."

Clint smirked, tipped his hat toward Rosie's and said, "I was just thinking the same thing."

Even with the distance separating them, Clint and Mace stared each other down as if they were seconds away from locking horns. In those seconds, it seemed to Clint as though the entire town was holding its breath so they could see which of them would waver first.

When Mace turned away and continued walking into the club, Clint looked around at the other men sharing the porch with him. Although the people on the street and boardwalks hadn't really noticed the stare down, the old men outside the general store certainly did.

Larry broke the silence with a laugh that wasn't quite as boisterous as his normal one. "Oh, Lordy! We heard about the scuffle outside of Rosie's and was kind of mad we missed it. Looks like we'll just have to wait around for the second show."

Clint got up from his chair and tipped his glass against his lips so he could drain the rest of his lemonade. The cold liquid trickled down his throat to take a bit of the edge from the heat that had been building throughout the day. He set down the glass and checked the street around him.

There were no other gunmen or familiar faces, but he knew they'd be coming soon enough.

"I'm not here to stir up any trouble," Clint said.

"Maybe, but yer not the type to run away from it, neither."

Clint looked over to Larry and studied the older man only to find that he was being studied right back.

"We see plenty of men wearing their guns and strutting up and down these streets," Larry said. "Hell, some of us used to do some strutting in our day as well.

"You're not stupid, Clint. Sitting out here and watching them fellas rather than charging in there like a bull proved that well enough. Just be sure to keep thinking straight. Don't let some asshole like Gilliam get to you. His men have spilled a lot of blood and Gilliam's done his fair share of damage as well. We've watched them carry the bodies out of there."

"I'll keep that in mind. Thanks."

One of the other men sitting behind Larry hadn't said a word the entire afternoon. That is, he hadn't spoken until this very moment. "But don't take no shit off of him, neither," he groused.

"Don't worry about that," Clint said. "I'd say it's time to give some back rather than take any more."

After a moment of glances being swapped between the old men, they all broke into laughter and raised their glasses. Clint couldn't even get one step away from that porch before shaking every one of the grizzled hands being offered to him.

TWENTY-SEVEN

Clint headed back to the Comfort Arms Hotel, hoping that all he would find there was a note from Wilbur. Then again, the more he thought about it, the more he hoped that Wilbur hadn't just walked right up to the place without checking on it from a distance first.

Before Clint could get too wrapped up in possibilities, he was at the hotel and approaching the front desk. The owner was behind it and, judging by the look on his face, he wasn't at all happy to see Clint.

"Your room's in no shape to be rented," the owner said.

"That's all right. I wasn't planning on staying—"

"Good," the owner interrupted. "Because I've had your things brought down here for you. There's the matter of the bill, as well."

Clint saw his saddlebags get pushed from behind the desk and when he looked up again, he was staring at a folded slip of paper. The owner held the paper in between his fingers, waving it impatiently until Clint took it from him.

"I'm sure you'll find everything's in order."

Clint laughed and handed the paper right back. "There seems to be a mistake. It looks like I'm getting charged for

113

a month or two worth of stays rather than the couple days I was here."

Looking over at the bill, the owner snorted, "That's for damages to the room. They're quite extensive."

"They sure are. The only problem is that I didn't damage that room. Why don't you send this bill over to Mr. Gilliam at Rosie's? He's the one that ought to pay it."

The owner winced in reaction to hearing the exact words he'd been hoping to avoid. He took the bill from Clint as his shoulders nearly sank all the way down to his knees. "Fine. I'll mark off the charges for the damages. Here," he said while handing the bill back to Clint. "That should be more to your liking."

Shaking his head, Clint took the bill and looked it over. It was still a bit more than he figured he should pay, but he settled up anyhow. Clint had to give the owner some credit for trying to recoup his losses. Both men knew that a snowball would sprout in hell before Gilliam paid for anyone's broken door.

"Thank you for your stay at the Comfort Arms," the owner said without even trying to sound convincing. "Oh, and one more thing. There's a message for you."

Before Clint could say anything, there was another folded slip of paper being handed to him. "Who brought this here?" he asked.

"Some young lady," was the offhanded reply. "I really didn't pay attention since I've got much more pressing matters to worry about."

"Do you at least recall when it was delivered?"

"Less than an hour ago."

It was obvious that the hotel's owner wasn't going to say anything else unless the words were physically dragged from him. Since Clint didn't need to hear anything that badly, he picked up his saddlebags and left the Comfort Arms.

Keeping the folded paper in his hand, Clint was sure to put some distance between himself and the hotel before stopping to see what had been written on it. Every second he was near that hotel, Clint felt like he was standing with a boulder teetering over his head.

He hadn't seen anyone watching the place, but he was certain that someone was either doing so from afar or would be coming by at any moment. Gilliam had made too big of a move for him to just sit back and forget about it. With all the activity he'd seen in and around Rosie's, Clint was certain that something was brewing.

He was also certain that he was right in the middle of it.

A couple of streets down, Clint finally picked a shady storefront where he could set his bags down and take a moment to read the note. With his back to a wall, Clint unfolded the paper and held it so he could also spot any nearby movement headed in his direction.

The note said: "Mason's. East side of town."

Short and sweet.

At least something turned out to be simple during this visit. At this point, Clint was grateful for anything he could get.

After refolding the note and sticking it in his pocket, Clint got moving once again. He needed to find somewhere to stay himself. Fortunately, it wouldn't be for much longer.

TWENTY-EIGHT

Clint headed east. He'd covered enough ground within Los Tejanos for him to be familiar with the town, but he didn't know every inch of it by heart. That was why he didn't think to question the name of the place where Wilbur was staying when he'd read it on the note.

He did think to question it, however, when he realized that there was no place called Mason's. Having walked from one end of the east side to the other without getting anything but a callus on his heel, Clint realized he was going to have to start looking for more than a hotel or boardinghouse.

When he came to a stop in front of a squat building on the outskirts of Los Tejanos, Clint dropped his saddlebags and started laughing to himself. The building looked like a brick with a few windows cut into the sides and was wedged into the ground as if it had fallen off the side of a wagon.

Its front was open to reveal a covered work space. The floor was covered in grit and gravel, and all of the interior walls that could be seen were covered with shelves holding hammers, spikes and chisels of all shapes and sizes.

"Are you the mason?" Clint asked once he'd caught the

attention of a burly man wearing a dark brown smock, with his sleeves rolled up to reveal a set of massive forearms.

The man swiped at the rivers of sweat pouring over his bald head and nodded. His grip tightened around the hammer in his hand as he said, "Yeah. And who might you be?"

"Clint Adams. I think some friends of mine might be waiting for me here."

Relief jumped onto the man's face as he set down his hammer. He walked around the stone he'd been carving and offered to shake Clint's hand. "Sorry about the reception just now. Wilbur's got some bad types after him. Well, badder than normal you might say. I guess you know all about that."

"I sure do."

"He's straight back through there," the mason said as he pointed to a narrow door that Clint had missed completely when he'd glanced over the inside of the squat building the first time. "Better announce yerself before going in. Him and the missus are a bit jumpy."

"That's understandable. Has anyone else come by today looking for them?"

"Nope," the mason replied without hesitation. "And I've been looking for 'em, too. I heard about all that's been happening lately, so I know Wilbur's got himself into a mess. Then again, it ain't no real surprise though."

"It isn't?"

"Eh, he's always been trying his luck. Sometimes he gives up, but he always comes back again. Usually he can pay back what he owes. This time, I think Gilliam's got him on his list."

"What list is that?"

"The list of folks who're working for him whether they like it or not," the mason said. Turning back to his work, the big man added, "Probably just after Wilbur's uncle Roy."

"Who's his uncle Roy?"

Stopping as though he thought he hadn't heard the question correctly, the mason hefted his hammer like he was lifting a twig and brought it down hard enough to crack the stone in front of him in half. "You don't know his uncle Roy? He's a big landowner up north. Runs one of the biggest logging companies in that part of the country."

Now things were starting to make a lot more sense. A man like Gilliam could possibly be pushing folks around for power, but getting his hooks into a bigger fish made a lot more sense.

"Thanks for everything," Clint said. "Hope it wasn't too much trouble."

The mason shrugged. "I been doing my best to steer clear of Gilliam since I set up my shop here. After all the shit that he's pulled over the years, I don't mind seeing some of it get flung right back into his face."

"Anyone ever bring the sheriff into it?" Clint asked.

"Who? Donner? He's about as useful as tits on a bull."

"Looks like meeting him once was all I needed," Clint grumbled. His words were lost amid the crunch of hammer against stone as the mason started chipping his slab down to size as though he was whittling down a twig.

Clint walked toward the back of the room and found that the door could have been even more well hidden than it already was. Its handle blended in almost perfectly with the tools hanging around it and the rest was covered with fully stocked shelves. It was slightly ajar, however, and opened easily upon well-oiled hinges.

The next room was a simple, square-shaped space. Compared to the room Clint had just left behind, this one looked positively empty. There was a cot, a few chairs and a table which appeared to be used as a desk. There were papers and a few books on the table, as well as a lantern which was lit just enough to illuminate the room.

Wilbur jumped up from the chair he'd been sitting in and froze until he could make out enough of Clint's face to recognize him. "Oh thank God it's you," Wilbur said. "I was beginning to think that someone caught on to the note I sent you. Did it get delivered all right?"

"I'm here, aren't I?" Clint replied.

"Oh yeah. Good point."

Clint's eyes were already drawn to the other person inside the room. She was a beauty who still managed to be stunning no matter what chaos was boiling around her.

"This is my wife, Daisy," Wilbur said.

Her smile practically lit up the room, but she only came close enough to step up to Wilbur's side. "Pleased to meet you," she said. "Thank you for stepping in on my husband's behalf."

Clint reached into his pocket and then extended that hand out to Wilbur. "Here. I think this belongs to you."

If her smile had been bright before, it was blinding when she saw her husband take his ring back and slip it onto his finger.

TWENTY-NINE

By the end of the day, people were thinking about anything but what had happened outside of Rosie's. In fact, once the sun had gone down and the liquor started to flow in earnest, people couldn't even come up with a good reason to keep their distance from the place.

With the darkness, there came a coolness to the air which made it even better for folks to wander the streets. Pianos were playing, dancers were dancing and voices were being raised. All of these noises and more blended together to replace the normal sounds that filled a desert night.

As the entire street got rowdier, there were a few at the eye of the hurricane who wanted nothing more than to escape the revelry. One such person huddled in her room, doing her best to ignore the repeated attempts to draw her out.

"Come on, sweetie," Kathy said through the door while rapping her knuckles against the frame. "There's some fella out here who want to see you."

Estrella sat in her room, perched on her bed, looking out at the street below. "Tell him to go away!" she shouted toward the door. Although she'd done a good job so far, she knew that she wouldn't be able to hold out much longer.

She'd already drawn enough attention to herself. Any more, and things would start to get painful.

Outside her door, Kathy fretted before trying the handle one more time. As before, the door was still locked. Suddenly, she spotted someone emerging from her office and she waved for him to come to her.

"Is Mr. Gilliam still up there?" she asked.

O'Shea didn't give an answer one way or the other. "Why you need to know?" he asked.

"Because he told me that Estrella wanted to entertain some paying customers."

"Yeah. And?"

"Well, she certainly doesn't act like it. If she just wants to be a hostess, that's fine. She's pretty enough to draw in a crowd. I won't have girls taking in other clients unless—"

"She'll do whatever you tell her to. If not, I'll knock her into shape myself."

"It doesn't work that way. Not on my watch."

"It don't matter whose watch it is. Mr. Gilliam wants her working on her back and that's all there is to it." Looking toward a young man wearing a rumpled suit, O'Shea asked, "Is that the fella who wants to take her for a ride?"

Although she obviously didn't like the sound of that, Kathy nodded. "Yes. He's the gentleman who would like to pay Estrella a visit."

"And she's putting up a fuss?"

Leaning in so she could drop her voice to a whisper, Kathy explained, "She won't even open her door."

O'Shea pushed Kathy aside and stomped down the hall. When he got to her door, he slammed his fist against it once. "Open up, Estrella. Now!"

The young man standing nearby fidgeted from one foot to another. Although he couldn't come close to hiding his nervousness, he clutched his money in his hand and remained planted in his spot.

Letting out an impatient breath, O'Shea pulled his arm

back as though he meant to punch a hole straight through the door. Before he could do anything of the sort, the door opened in front of him and Estrella stepped into view.

She wore a black dress with a neckline that plunged deep enough to show her ample cleavage. Her skin was the color of lightly creamed coffee and her hair fell around her face in thick waves. Her eyes remained locked on O'Shea until the big gunman backed down. From there, she looked to Kathy.

"Are you all right?" Kathy asked.

While Estrella had plenty she wanted to say to Kathy, she knew none of it would do any good. The woman had been kind enough to her, but she was an employee of Mr. Gilliam and tended to believe most of what he told to her. Having O'Shea looming over all three of them cut Estrella's odds even further.

Rather than say any of the things that were going through her mind at that moment, Estrella clasped her hands in front of herself and put on a smile. "Sorry," she said. "I was having some trouble with my lock."

Kathy looked from Estrella to O'Shea and then back to Estrella. "Are you sure that's all it was?"

Estrella nodded. Before any more questions could be asked, she set her eyes upon the young man in the rumpled suit and held out her hand. "You must be the man Kathy was talking about."

Just having Estrella talk directly to him was enough to make the young man forget everything that had come before. His face broke into a goofy smile and he walked straight up to her as though O'Shea wasn't even there.

"Glad to meet you," the young man said. When he was led into Estrella's room, whatever else he'd wanted to say was quickly forgotten.

"You sure there's no more problem here?" O'Shea asked.

Estrella nodded. "I guess I was just a little nervous."

Kathy started to say something, but heard her name being called from the nearby lounge. "Then I guess I'll leave you two alone," she said. "Just let me know if you need anything."

Satisfied that he'd put the situation away for good, O'Shea gave Estrella a leering smile and walked down the hall himself.

Estrella closed the door and turned to find the young man deciding whether he should sit on the bed or walk up closer to her. When he'd decided on the latter, she turned away from him and stepped to the window.

Just then, she spotted something outside that made her smile shine with a genuine fire. "You want some fresh air?" she asked. Before the young man could answer, she'd already opened the window as wide as it could go.

Without another word, she looked at the young man, winked and then hopped out through the window.

THIRTY

Clint had been wandering around Rosie's for a couple of minutes before he found the correct window. Once he spotted Estrella through the glass, he'd waved and hoped to catch her attention. He did that just fine, and got a whole lot more of a reaction besides.

When he saw her throw open the window, Clint wanted to signal for her to meet him in the alley next to the club. He managed to get out the first part of the first word before he saw her step out of the window and onto the overhanging ledge just outside her room.

Running forward on instinct, Clint held out his hands as though that would be enough to save her if she happened to slip. Estrella, on the other hand, didn't seem to have a fear in the world. On the contrary, she walked on that ledge as though it was solid ground and she smiled down at him like he was an entire regiment of cavalry.

As Clint rushed forward to help while Estrella made her way down from the ledge, he looked around to see how many others were watching. She was climbing out through a window at the side of the building, which was mostly in the dark. The people that were coming and going from Rosie's were either too focused on what waited for them inside or weren't too concerned with what was going on over their heads.

Estrella, on the other hand, didn't seem to be concerned with anything at all, apart from Clint. She walked quickly along the ledge and onto the overhang of the first floor's roof. From there, she stepped onto an awning made from wooden slats.

All the while, she didn't pause or give one thought about the possibility of falling. The only thing that seemed to concern her at all was that she get closer to Clint.

For a moment, Clint thought he was literally going to have to catch her. When Estrella made it to the edge of the awning, she stopped at the last possible second so she could sit and dangle her legs over the side. Without another moment's hesitation, she slid off and dropped toward the ground.

Thankfully, she only had about seven feet to fall and Clint didn't have to catch her completely. He did rush forward with his arms outstretched to keep her from breaking a leg or snapping an ankle. The moment she landed, Estrella wrapped her arms around him and let out an excited squeal.

"Oh, Clint, I was starting to think you weren't going to come."

"I may be a little late, but I made it here," he replied. "Actually, I didn't think you'd be literally jumping out of your window."

She looked at him and gave him another hug. "I don't have much choice, especially with someone in my room and more waiting outside my door."

"Wait a minute," Clint said as his eyes darted up to look at the window that was still hanging open on the second floor. "You mean there was someone in your room?"

"Well, yes."

"How long do you think they'll wait before telling anyone that you left him there all by himself?"

"Oh, I don't know. We've probably got at least—"

She was cut short by the sound of a voice shouting from above their heads. Sure enough, an excited face poked out from Estrella's window and started searching the street below.

Clint grabbed hold of her and pulled her closer to the building. Even though they were quickly beneath the awning, Clint didn't take too much comfort from their position.

"I was kind of hoping you'd manage something a little quieter than this," he said.

The smile on Estrella's face was too wide and too bright to be contained. She looked up and then back at him before shrugging. "Sorry. This is my first time escaping from somewhere. Well, that is unless you take my hometown into account, but that was a little different."

"Yeah. Running away from home doesn't usually require dodging a bullet."

"What?"

"Never mind. Do you know a quick way for us to get out of sight?"

Still holding Clint tightly, Estrella nodded toward a dark section of the street. "There's some alleyways and plenty of doorways down there. I checked it out myself."

"Then I'll take your word for it," Clint said as he took her by the hand and started moving toward the darker section of street.

Noises were starting to grow louder from the vicinity of Rosie's. Namely, the noises of angry voices mentioning Estrella by name or description. At the very least, Clint took some degree of comfort from the fact that those voices were a good ways behind them and still seemed pretty confused.

A few people burst out of Rosie's and started to spread out from there. Clint could tell that much just by listening to the slamming of doors and the stomping of boots against the boardwalk. He didn't let any of those things slow him down as he and Estrella kept racing for the cover of shadows.

Clint felt much better when he made it to a spot that was so dark that he couldn't even see the path in front of him. Although he didn't want to risk running any farther, that meant that anyone pursuing him couldn't see much of anything, either.

"So you scouted this out, huh?" Clint asked.

Already, Estrella was pressed up tightly against him. As the voices and footsteps fanned out into the streets, she pressed in even tighter. Clint could smell the scent of her hair as well as the faint sweetness of her skin. The warmth of her body was more than enough to cancel the cold of the desert night and make him feel like it was high noon all over again.

"I looked real carefully," she whispered. "You'll just have to trust me."

As the voices drew closer and the footsteps became louder, Clint figured he didn't really have any other choice.

THIRTY-ONE

Although it was easy enough to tell that the voices belonged to a bunch of angry men, Clint only recognized one of them. He was certain that O'Shea was among the fellows in the street looking for Estrella, which was enough to tell him that the rest of the men had to work for Gilliam as well.

Clint and Estrella huddled together in the cold embrace of shadows. His hand inched down for the gun at his side and froze when a couple of sets of footsteps came to a stop no more than five or six feet away from him.

"She just jumped out the window?" O'Shea asked.

"Near as I can tell," another man replied. "That's what the kid in her room was saying."

"Well, it's not too bad of a jump, and since nobody saw her come down the stairs I guess that has to be the case."

"So what do we do now? Keep lookin' till we find her?"

O'Shea let out an aggravated grunt. "If she was hurt in the fall, we would'a seen her already. Since she ain't around, that means she must've gotten away."

O'Shea stopped talking and took a few steps toward the shadowed alleyway. Clint didn't move anything apart from the muscles required to shift his eyes in their sockets. Peering through a veil of Estrella's hair, he could just make out the other man's silhouette as it drew closer to where he was hiding.

The breath froze on its way into Clint's lungs. In his arms, he could feel Estrella's body tensing. Although the situation was potentially deadly, Clint couldn't help but be a little distracted by the way she slowly pushed and writhed against his body.

Just when it seemed that O'Shea had picked them out, the gunman slammed his fist against the wall not too far from Clint's head and snarled, "Aw, to hell with this. If Mr. Gilliam needs that bitch around so bad, he can find her himself."

With that, O'Shea turned and stomped back into Rosie's. The man with him asked some questions, but the words were lost once they both got back into the swell of the club's crowd.

Estrella turned to look Clint in the eyes, making sure to keep her face within an inch or two of his. "That was close," she said in an excited whisper.

"It sure was. Good thing you wore this black dress. Anything else and we would be in the middle of a fight right about now."

"Yeah. Good thing."

Despite the words she said, Clint had no trouble picking up the disappointment laying just beneath them. He started to move out of the shadow to get a better look in the street when he was stopped by Estrella's arm blocking his way.

"Where do you think you're going?" she asked.

Clint looked at her and, even in the deep shadows, could make out the glimmer of excitement still illuminating her features.

"We need to get out of here," he said. "There's a place not too far where we can hide for a bit."

Estrella's smile curled into a pouting frown. "But we're plenty hidden right here." She took hold of Clint's gun belt and started pulling him deeper into the alley. "Those men that were looking for us already went back inside."

Since it seemed that she was right and the street was already quieting down, Clint allowed himself to be pulled along with her into the alley. The night was getting colder by the minute, but the heat of their bodies was feeding off of each other and growing just as quickly.

She had hold of both of Clint's hands by this point and was positioning him so he was always in front of her and his back was against the wall. As she passed in and out of the shadows, the pale light from the stars and moon played down the front of her body. The red ribbons threaded among the black material of her dress looked almost wet in the moonlight.

"All the time I've been working for Mr. Gilliam, I never once did what he wanted me to do," she said. "I served drinks and flirted with all the rich men, but I didn't share my bed with any of them."

Since she'd brought his hands so close to her body, Clint found himself placing them upon her hips and feeling the way they swayed as she walked and pushed him against the wall. "That's good," he replied, allowing his hands to wander up and down over her hips and then up toward her waist.

Estrella smiled and kept her eyes locked on to his, but never once moved to keep his hands from traveling over her body. "Even when Mr. Gilliam insisted I started sharing my bed with them, I always thought of a way out of it. But that doesn't mean I'm made of stone.

"I see men come in there who I might want to spend some time with. When I heard someone mention your name and that you were in town, I wanted to see you for myself. Now that I have," she added, pausing to let her eyes move up and down over Clint's chest, "I'm real glad I get to have you all to myself."

Clint's body was reacting to her closeness. She felt the

erection growing between his legs and rubbed herself against him as the warmth of her skin flowed from beneath the layers of her clothing. The more Clint felt of her, the more he wanted to feel. Her hips were round and firm and she let out a small gasp as the edges of his fingers brushed along the sides of her breasts.

"This may not be the best time, you know," he said, even as his hands teased her nipples which became harder beneath his touch.

"But I want you so bad, Clint. This is all I've been thinking about. I've been waiting for this all day long."

Clint shifted against the wall so he could easily look down either end of the alley. They were in a spot where any little noise that came up rattled between either of the buildings closing them in. "Someone might find us," he said, feeling her heart pound against his hand.

"I don't care," she said, already pulling open his belt and then his jeans. "And if you cared, you wouldn't be doing what you're doing to me right now."

"What do you mean?" Clint asked before grasping both breasts in his hands and massaging them firmly. "Is this what you're talking about?"

"Yes," Estrella said breathlessly. "God, yes."

THIRTY-TWO

She had his pants opened and was reaching inside them before Clint could say another word. Her fingers quickly found his rigid penis and wrapped around it so she could start rubbing it in long strokes.

Clint wasn't able to pull the top part of her dress down too far because of the way it was cinched tightly against her body. He was, however, able to get one hand underneath her skirts so he could feel the warm, soft skin beneath them.

Estrella's thighs were thick with muscle and Clint could feel them start to tremble as he ran his hands along the smooth skin. Every so often, his fingers would brush against a bit of lace. The wisps of fabric beneath her skirts were warm from the heat of her skin and clinging to her flesh.

As Clint slid both hands under her skirts and found various spots to touch her, Estrella was busy as well. She now had one foot propped up on the wall so she could spread her legs open a bit more and press herself against him from an even better angle. This way, she made it easier for Clint to rub the moist lips between her thighs while she continued to stroke his cock and make his erection grow even harder.

The sounds from outside the alley still drifted through the air, but neither one of them was really hearing them. Although Clint was doing his best to keep alert to anyone who might approach, he wasn't having much luck focusing on anything else. There wasn't anyone approaching the alley. Even if someone did happen to look in that direction, all they would see was one blob of darkness moving inside another.

Estrella's black dress wrapped around them like a smoky blanket. Within the satin, lace and ribbons, she and Clint were drawing closer and closer until one of them made the move that they'd both been waiting for.

Clint's fingers had slipped beneath her lace panties to brush along the warm thatch of hair beneath them. Now that she had one foot up against the wall, all he needed to do was pull those panties aside and push her skirts up just high enough for him to get under there with her.

Estrella let out a sigh that was almost loud enough to be heard outside the alley when she felt Clint's cock between her legs. She closed her eyes, leaned her head back slightly and guided him into her. Once his rigid shaft slid between her moist, waiting lips, she wrapped both arms around his neck and took every inch of him inside of her.

It took every bit of willpower Clint had to keep himself from making a noise louder than hers. Estrella's pussy was so wet and so warm that he thought his knees might buckle before he got all the way inside. He held up just fine, however, since Estrella was all but pushing him up against the wall.

Once Clint's hands were cupping her firm, rounded backside, they both fell into a rhythm that made the previous sensations pale by comparison. As Clint moved in and out of her, Estrella pumped her hips in quick little motions at just the right time to make them both light-headed.

Clint kept his hands on her buttocks so he could feel every move she made. He was even able to guide her when he wanted to slide all the way inside and stay there for a moment without moving. In those moments, he took a quick look around to see if anyone had spotted them. When he looked back, Estrella was smiling broadly.

"It's like we're all alone in here," she whispered. Grinding her hips slowly, she looked up at the night sky and purred, "God, Clint, this is the best I've felt in a long time."

Clint didn't need to say anything in response. His expression resembled that of a man who'd drunk just enough to make him forget his troubles and that was all Estrella needed to see. She looked the same way, in fact. Both of them were wrapped in her cloud of black lace and making love under the stars.

It just didn't get much better than that.

Even as that thought passed through Clint's mind, he was proven wrong.

Estrella kept one hand around the back of Clint's neck as she used the other to run her fingertips over his chest. From there, she leaned back as far as her arm would allow while thrusting her hips in a motion that both led him and begged Clint for more at the same time.

Following her lead, Clint began pumping into her with more force until she was grunting with pleasure every time their bodies came together. He went even further by reaching down and picking her up just enough so he could turn her around and push her back against the wall.

Estrella landed with a surprised huff, her eyes growing wide as saucers. Her mouth opened as though she meant to say something to him, but her breath was stolen from her when Clint began to slide his entire length in and out of her. Now, it was her turn to follow his lead and she reached around with both arms to hang on and enjoy the ride.

First, Clint felt one of her legs wrap tightly around his waist. Then, Estrella's other leg came up to slide around him. Her ankles were locked tightly at the small of his back and she used both legs to move her hips in time to Clint's motions.

All that could be heard in the darkness was the rustle of Estrella's skirts and their combined breathing which was becoming heavier by the second. Clint was lost in his own world, yet also felt as though his senses were also sharper than ever.

In the moments before his climax came, the shadows seemed less dark. He thought he could even hear every note played on a nearby piano. Estrella's eyes were clenched shut, but she had the same expression of profound pleasure etched across her face. She pulled in short, quick breaths, which Clint could feel in a way that made it hard for him to breathe as well.

Finally, after one more powerful thrust, both of them were overtaken by orgasms which nearly caused them to break the silence in a way that would most definitely be noticed. Clint's knees were shaking, but he held her up just long enough for Estrella to collect herself and stand on her own two feet.

"Good Lord," she whispered.

Clint pulled in a breath. "Yeah. I was just thinking the same thing."

"That almost makes me want to go back in there so you can rescue me again."

"Oh no, you don't. I've got somewhere else in mind that should be a whole lot safer."

THIRTY-THREE

The next morning dawned, but there wasn't a bit of sunlight to mark it. Clouds had rolled in thick enough to cover the sky with a dark gray blanket and the occasional flash of lightning. It was going to be one of those storms that hung on for a while and everyone inside the remote cabin knew it. After living most of their lives in the desert, knowing such things had become second nature.

While the cabin was a fairly good size, there were enough people inside of it to make it feel cramped. Besides Clint and Estrella, there was also Wilbur and Daisy, bringing the number of people inside the cabin to roughly twice of what was intended.

Thunder rolled through the air, shaking the cabin right along with everything laying on a table or resting in a cabinet. Tin plates and cups clattered together and when the rain started to fall, it wasn't long before little streams dripped from between the shingles upon the roof.

"It's gonna be a hell of a storm," Wilbur said, stretching his neck to look at the ceiling over his head as though he could see straight through to the sky. "We could use it."

Daisy nodded from her spot next to her husband. "Yep. We sure can."

136

Ever since Clint and Estrella had arrived at the cabin the night before, things had been more than a little tense. Apart from everything else that had happened, Estrella wasn't exactly made to feel welcome. Daisy looked at her with disdain and smacked Wilbur on the back of the head when he started to be a little more accommodating.

Clint had made the introductions and brought everyone up to speed on their situations, but that didn't do anything to ease the edge in Daisy's voice. Rather than try to make her feel better, Clint had picked a spot in a corner where he could see both front and back doors and went to sleep. Unfortunately, things weren't much better in the morning.

"Did this roof always leak?" Estrella asked.

"Yes," Daisy grunted. "My family wasn't some bunch of rich saloon owners or . . ." She gave Estrella yet another disapproving glare before adding, ". . . entertainers."

Clint ignored the tension crackling between the two women and stretched his back and arms while rubbing the sleep from his eyes. "Leaks aren't our biggest concern. How many others know about this place?"

Anxious to avoid the confrontation and stay out of Daisy's reach, Wilbur replied, "Not many that we should worry about."

"I'm sure Gilliam asked about any land holdings you may have once he started coming after his money."

Although Daisy looked at him disapprovingly, Wilbur nodded. "Yeah. He did. But I never told him about this place. It's not mine to give."

That seemed to make Daisy feel a little better. Within the last twelve hours, she'd been forced to deal with the ugliest part of her husband's loss at the card table. Every new trouble hit her harder than the last until she finally started wearing a frown and walking like she had a weight upon her shoulders.

"You think anyone would tell Gilliam about this place?" Clint asked just to be certain. "Even in passing?"

Wilbur and Daisy both thought about it before they started shaking their heads.

"All right then. What about you?" Clint asked, looking over to Estrella. "Do you think anyone besides Gilliam would be looking for you or have any chance of tracking you down anytime soon?"

"Not that I can think of. Then again," she added with a mischievous smirk, "I was a little preoccupied after my rescue."

"Good Lord," Daisy murmured just loud enough for everyone to hear. "Please don't force us to listen to all the sordid details."

Estrella's eyes flared and she turned to look squarely at the other woman. "And just what is that supposed to mean?"

"It means that when you're not a whore getting everything handed to you, it's possible you might have to spend a night or two under a leaky roof."

All it took was the first couple words of that statement to spur Clint and Wilbur into action. Both men hustled across the room and put themselves in between the women. Wilbur was just in time to push his wife back into her chair and Clint was just in time to catch Estrella as she started to charge toward her.

"We've got enough problems without fighting amongst ourselves, ladies," Clint said in a diplomatic voice that was still loud enough to be heard.

"I'm thankful for all your help, Clint," Daisy said. "That's why I've come out here on a moment's notice and put my life on hold. I'm a patient woman, which is why I've stuck by my husband throughout all of this. But I will not live under the same roof as a known whore!"

Clint had Estrella in his arms and tightened his grip around her when he heard that. Even so, it almost wasn't enough to keep her from rushing over to tear Daisy apart.

"You don't know me," Estrella seethed. "You can't talk like that to me!"

"I've heard plenty," Daisy countered. "And it's enough to—"

"Enough to what?" Clint interrupted. "Enough to waste your time screaming and fighting like children when there are men out there looking to tear your lives apart?"

Clint looked between the women and saw that his words had struck home equally with them both. Just to be certain, he went on to say, "Gilliam doesn't like to lose what he thinks is his. I've seen plenty of men like him to recognize that much. I can also see that he thinks he owns all three of you."

"So what happens now?" Wilbur asked. "Do we hide here and hope that Mr. Gilliam forgets about us?"

Both of the women turned to see what Clint had to say in response to that. They were interested in it enough to forget about the punches they'd been ready to throw.

"There's no chance of him forgetting about any of this," Clint said deviously. "So I propose that we make him regret the day he ever met you."

THIRTY-FOUR

"Three days," Gilliam fumed as he paced a rut into the floor over Kathy's head. "It's been three days and I'm supposed to believe that not one of you men have seen hide nor hair of any one of those three?"

Although the men lined up in Gilliam's office weren't all of the killers on his payroll, they represented the highest ranking of them. At the moment, however, the gunmen looked more like boys summoned to the schoolmaster rather than a collection of hired killers.

Gilliam had that effect on people; especially when he stomped back and forth with his hand swinging dangerously close to his own holstered pistol. There was a fire in his eyes that brought his sanity into question. When he spoke, Gilliam bared his teeth like an animal that was searching for an unprotected jugular.

"Well?" Gilliam snarled. "Who's going to answer for this?"

Of the men lined up in the office, one of them seemed as though he was more inconvenienced than intimidated. That man was one of the older ones and he was only known as Mace.

"They're with Adams," Mace said.

Gilliam nodded slowly as he walked over to stand directly in front of Mace. "Oh. You know that for a fact, do you?"

"It makes sense. They've been on their own up until now and haven't done so well. We all saw Adams standing up for Wilbur Johanssen right in this very office. Since Wilbur's dumber than a hitching post, I'd say that any smart move sure as hell wasn't his idea."

Standing right next to Mace, O'Shea started nodding as well. "Yeah. And wherever Wilbur goes, he takes that pretty little wife of his right along with him."

Gilliam stepped in front of O'Shea, still keeping his hands close to the pistol at his side. His gray hair was rumpled after three restless nights of sleep. His face was red from shouting and his voice was even more ragged than usual. "And I suppose you'd buy into that explanation in regards to the whore as well? That would be convenient seeing as how you were the one that was supposed to keep her in line."

Before O'Shea could answer, the Chinese girl who rarely left the office slipped up to Gilliam's side to offer him the rink he'd been working on. O'Shea glanced to her and shrugged. "All due respect, Mr. Gilliam, but you got other whores."

Without a pause or a single glance over his shoulder, Gilliam snapped his right arm straight out and back just enough to knock the Chinese girl off her feet. "You mean her?" he asked without even looking at the damage he'd caused to the Chinese girl's face. "She's not the one I was asking about, was I?"

"No."

"Then stop talking about her. She's obedient, but she's not blind or deaf. She's like all the other girls in here who are just like all the ones out there," he said, stabbing a finger toward the window overlooking the rest of the town. "Women talk to each other and they know every little thing that goes on. They'll know that one of my girls defied me and now the rest of them will start getting ideas to do the same. The ones out there will start spreading the word that I'm getting soft. I can't have that."

O'Shea looked down at the Chinese girl who was struggling to get to her feet. It wasn't until just then that he realized he'd never even known her name.

Mace had yet to even acknowledge the girl's presence. His eyes remained pointed either forward or at Gilliam. "So you think Adams had something to do with Estrella getting away from us?"

"Didn't you say that she pulled him aside the first time he was in here?" Gilliam asked.

Mace nodded.

"Then, yeah. I'll bet that he had something to do with her leaving." Suddenly, Gilliam stopped short and fixed his eyes upon O'Shea. His face twisted into an angry mask that only got worse when he saw that O'Shea was starting to reach out to help the Chinese girl to her feet. Without a moment's hesitation, Gilliam's hand dropped down to pluck the gun from his holster.

"I've had it with my men not taking this seriously," Gilliam seethed. With that, he aimed his gun and pulled the trigger.

The room filled with the thunder of the shot, which echoed within the enclosed space after rattling everything inside of it. For a second or two, nobody moved. Then, as smoke began curling up from Gilliam's barrel, a muted grunt drifted through the air.

Still trying to stand up, the Chinese girl reached up with one hand to press it against the bloody hole that had just been blown through her chest. She tried to pull in a breath but failed. She tried to stay on her feet, but quickly dropped onto her side.

Her eyes fluttered and yet she still kept from crying out as if she thought even that would offend her employer.

O'Shea had moved to draw out of reflex, but stayed his hand before clearing leather. He forced himself to look away from the Chinese girl only after she let out her last breath and crumpled into a lifeless husk.

A subtle twitch passed over Mace's features, but not much else.

"There," Gilliam said. He kept his pistol drawn, making it clear that he would fire again if the mood struck him. "You think you can concentrate on what needs to be done?"

O'Shea straightened up and nodded solemnly. "Yessir."

"Good. We already missed Adams once and everyone saw the bodies of my men getting dragged from that hotel. You think Mark Bradshaw didn't see that? You think he doesn't know what happened? I can't have a powerful man like that thinking I'm weak.

"We need to find Adams, Johanssen or that whore. Odds are that if we find one, we'll find at least one more from that list, so let's get to it."

"We've been asking around and looking for three days," O'Shea said.

"You've been looking for about a day and a half," Gilliam corrected. "And asking won't help. Johanssen's got friends that would lie for him and almost anyone around here knew that Estrella was one of my whores."

"Looking ain't enough." Since his voice was rarely heard, it made more of an impact when Mace actually spoke up.

Both O'Shea and Gilliam stopped what they were doing to hear what he said next.

"We need to do something to draw them out," Mace said.

O'Shea let out a snort of a laugh. "Sure. If any of them are still anywhere close to here."

Mace turned to look directly at O'Shea. The move was slow and deliberate. After no more than a second of direct eye contact, he was able to make O'Shea start shifting uncomfortably in his spot. Only after O'Shea lowered his eyes completely did Mace continue talking.

"Johanssen's still here," Mace said. "He's got nowhere else to go. I checked up on his family once we started putting the squeeze on him and he don't have any that he can get to. As for Adams, my guess is he ain't too far, either."

"Why do you say that?" Gilliam asked.

"Because we took our shot and missed. A man like him don't turn tail and run after something like that."

Gilliam nodded and finally allowed a smirk to cross his face. "You see? That's what I'm talking about. That's what I call thorough! Mace, tell me the rest of what's on your mind."

"What about me?" O'Shea asked.

With a dismissive wave toward the dead Chinese girl, Gilliam said, "Clean up that mess."

THIRTY-FIVE

It had been a rough couple of days for Clint.

That wasn't because of the accommodations, the time spent hiding out or even the fact that he knew Gilliam's men were out looking for everyone in the Johanssen's cabin. Mostly, it was rough because Clint wasn't able to enjoy one moment of peace and quiet throughout the entire time.

Having a bed was better than sleeping on the ground, but at least a campsite was fairly relaxing at times. Having the company of a woman was always good, but not when that woman was constantly ready to sink her claws into one of the other women in the same cabin.

Estrella and Daisy had been sniping at each other without once coming up for air. They kept it under their hats whenever possible, but that kind of subtle tension still filled the air with a crackle like the threat of lightning. Sometimes, Clint wanted one of them to just explode and be done with it. Unfortunately, he knew that as long as one of them was still drawing breath, the end was nowhere in sight.

One of the things that had been keeping him sane over those couple of days was that most of Clint's time was spent with Wilbur. He and Wilbur sat at the little dining table for hours at a time, going over strategies and plans. When he was done, Clint would start over and go through it again. After around the fourth or fifth time, Wilbur started to truly catch on.

Estrella had her own things to do and Daisy kept herself busy by making the meals and trying to do something close to her normal routine. Every time one of the women caught the other's eye, the comments would fly and the bickering would start all over again.

Finally, on the third day, Clint was outside the cabin for some fresh air when something occurred to him.

It was quiet.

Not only was it quiet, but it was actually peaceful.

There were no arguing voices or angry footsteps. There weren't even any comments that were grunted under someone's breath in a way that sounded more like the roar of flowing water than any sort of whisper. There was none of that.

Clint closed his eyes, pulled in an easy breath and savored it for as long as he possibly could.

As it turned out, that was for right around one minute.

"Clint? Can I talk to you for a second?"

It was Estrella's voice that had interrupted Clint's moment of peace. When he turned to see the casual smile on her face, he didn't really mind the interruption.

"What can I do for you?" he asked.

She had her arms crossed as she walked over to stand beside him. When she noticed that he was leaning against one of the posts that supported the front awning, she nestled in close to him and leaned back as well.

Leaning her head back so it rested against his shoulder, she said, "I'm frightened."

Although he could think of plenty of reasons for that, Clint wrapped one arm around her and asked, "What's frightening you?"

"I know you're here to protect us and all, but I still can't help but think what Gilliam or one of his men would do if they got their hands on me again. He keeps plenty of girls for his own and . . . I was supposed to be one of them. If one of those girls tried to get away or even refused him . . ." She let that trail off as a shudder worked its way through her body.

"If you'd rather just go, you can pick a direction and start riding any time you like."

He'd collected Eclipse as well as a few other horses not too long after they'd gotten to the cabin, which were all standing in a fenced area behind the building. Estrella glanced over in that direction, but only considered the notion for a few seconds.

"There's some places I could go, I suppose," she said. "But if Gilliam ever found out where I went, I don't even know what he'd do. Maybe nothing. Maybe . . ."

That shudder went through her again, making the rest of Estrella's words snag in her throat.

Taking hold of her so he could turn her around and look directly into Estrella's face, Clint said, "Your help would be appreciated, but you can go anytime you want. You've been held captive long enough."

She smiled and shot a glance toward the cabin. "What about them?" she asked. "They can't just ride off. Their home is here."

"If you want to go, I can work around it. The plan we've been working on can work with or without you. Actually, I've been thinking it through both ways just in case you wanted to put this place behind you. To tell you the truth, I wouldn't blame you if you did just that."

Estrella's smile returned. This time, however, it was as wide as when they'd been together in the shadows and it was brighter than the few rays of sunlight that managed to pierce the clouds. "It's been a long time since I had much say in what I do or where I go. Just knowing that the choice is there makes me feel like a free woman."

"You are free."

"Maybe now. But while a woman is with Gilliam, they might as well be slaves. It's either do what he wants or pay the price."

"Are all the girls there like that?"

"No. Plenty of them want to be there. There's good money to be made and Kathy knows how to run a place like that. Just the ones that get singled out by Mr. Gilliam are the ones who need to worry."

"Well you don't need to worry anymore, Estrella. If you do want to go, just tell me who the others are who don't want to be there so I can see about getting them out."

She leaned forward and planted a kiss on Clint's mouth that took his breath away. "No need for that. I think I'll tell them myself."

"Glad to hear it. Now let's get the others. I think it's about time we headed back into town."

THIRTY-SIX

When the day passed into night, the shift was hardly noticeable. After hours of overcast skies and gray light filtering down through thick layers of cloud, the blackness of night was almost a comfort. At least the sun was dipping below the horizon to keep from pumping any more heat through the clouds which made the heat all the more unbearable.

In the desert, night brought cold right along with it. The amount of cold might vary by the time of year, but the equation was still the same. It wasn't any different on this night. In fact, this night brought a certain type of cold with it that had nothing to do with the temperature.

It was the kind of chill that was felt inside a person's bones before it was felt on their skin. It was also the type of chill that couldn't be erased by coats or fire.

Clint could feel the cold rolling in throughout the entire time he'd spoken to Estrella, Wilbur and Daisy. As they discussed what they intended to do, their faces became grimmer and grimmer. But, no matter how nervous they were, not one of them thought of backing out. It was too late for that. Besides, there wasn't anything else left for them on the road they were traveling.

Clint brought Eclipse to a stop just before they entered town. "So, is everyone straight on what we're doing?"

There were nods all around.

"Good. Does anyone have any second thoughts?"

Silence.

Each of them rode their own horse. They fanned out and rode side by side as though they each wanted the town of Los Tejanos in their sights. After steeling themselves, they looked over to Clint for the final command.

"All right then," Clint said. "Let's go."

And with that, they went. Clint didn't mean for the parting to be so solemn. In truth, he'd taken each of them through the steps enough times for them to complete their tasks without putting themselves into too much danger.

Of course, he knew he wasn't dealing with experienced gun hands, so he didn't give any of them more than they could handle. It also wouldn't do to go through so much trouble just to take them from one dangerous spot and put them into another.

Daisy squeezed her husband's hand one more time before pointing her horse toward one side of town and flicking the reins. Wilbur watched her go and nodded as she was quickly swallowed up by the protective darkness.

Estrella wasn't quite so hesitant, but she did give Clint a smirk before she pointed her own horse toward a different street and got it moving.

"Well," Wilbur said. "I guess that leaves just us."

Clint nodded once. "You ready for this, Wilbur?"

"I don't have much to lose anymore."

Looking toward the path that Daisy had taken, Clint asked, "Are you so certain of that?"

"I won't do her any good if I'm dead. I just wanted you to know that the offer you gave to all of us on our way here stands for you, too. If you want to call this off, I can take care of it myself. Hell, I should'a done that from the beginning instead of letting it get this far."

Clint couldn't help but think about Mark Bradshaw just then. "If more people were so eager to take charge of things themselves, I doubt there'd be half the problems there are in this world. But you're not the problem, Wilbur.

"You're a good man who got in over his head. There's no reason for you to die for that. Besides," Clint added while flicking the reins to get Eclipse moving toward the main street of Los Tejanos, "this isn't about you and your wife anymore. Other people are getting hurt and I can't stand for that."

Both men were riding for the middle of town. Having set himself to the task at hand, Wilbur seemed much more at ease. He leaned over and said, "That's all fine and good, but Mr. Gilliam also sent those men to kill you. That had to piss you off something fierce."

Clint nodded slowly. He wasn't the type to go after someone just because they'd crossed his path. Then again, just because he wasn't a sinner, that didn't make him a saint.

"Like I said. This isn't just about you and your wife anymore."

THIRTY-SEVEN

When Clint made any sort of plan, the first thing he considered was what could go wrong. One of the first things on his list was that Gilliam would try to get to the Johanssens by going after whatever he could. That included anything that the couple held dear and hadn't taken with them when they'd followed Clint to their short escape in the cabin.

Having that in his mind at all times, Clint was able to figure out instantly what was going on when he saw one familiar man leading a few others in the direction of the Johanssen's house. The grim purpose in their eyes was clear.

The torches in their hands were even clearer.

"Hey, Wilbur. Didn't you mention once that Gilliam threatened to burn your house down if you didn't pay him?"

"Yeah."

Clint didn't say much of anything after that. He didn't need to. Wilbur had already spotted the men crossing the street just under two blocks away.

"Oh my God," Wilbur said as he fidgeted in his saddle.

Clint reached out to put a calming hand on Wilbur's arm. He was ready to hold on tight enough to keep the man from breaking away from him. "I know," he said quietly. "Looks like we're going to have a slight change of plans."

"What do you mean?" Wilbur asked frantically. "We were supposed to make it known that we were back. We were supposed to draw them out. They're heading for my house with them torches. That's got to be the place they're going."

Although he didn't want to worry him, Clint was pretty sure that this was one of the few occasions where the conclusion being jumped to was actually the right one. The men were being led by O'Shea and every last one of them was armed. Now that they'd all crossed the street, Clint counted four torches being carried around the next corner.

"We don't know that for certain," Clint said fairly convincingly.

"Well, whatever those fellas are going to do with them torches can't be good."

"I'll agree with you on that one. So let's not do anything just yet to make them think they've got anything to worry about." Pulling back on Eclipse's reins, Clint made certain that Wilbur did the same. "I don't think they've seen us yet."

Wilbur sucked in a breath and sat up straight. Spotting this immediately, Clint reached out and snatched the reins from his hands before Wilbur could follow up on the courage he'd just found.

"I've got a better idea," Clint said. "Just trust me."

He didn't give Wilbur a chance to reply. Eclipse was already leading the way down a shadowy side street.

THIRTY-EIGHT

O'Shea walked tall, glancing every so often at the locals nearby like a king surveying his subjects. He carried his torch in his left hand, making sure to keep his other hand free to draw his gun at any time. One of the other men walked beside him while the others followed behind.

"From what I hear, the Johanssens ain't even in town no more," the man next to O'Shea said.

"Then he'll have a real nice surprise when he gets back, won't he?"

The gunmen rounded the corner and could already see the little house situated in a row with some others not too much farther down the street. By the time they got to the Johanssen place, they'd acquired a small crowd to watch them.

All of the gunmen glared at their audience, but none of them played their part better than O'Shea. He walked right up to the front door and pounded on it with his fist even though he knew there was nobody home.

"Come on out, Wilbur," O'Shea said as though he was on a stage. "You need to pay your debts like every other honest man in this town."

There were grumbles from the crowd as folks tried to

get a grip on what they were seeing. A few of them split off to run in different directions, but most of them were unable to move their feet or take their eyes from the scene that was before them.

"You've had plenty of chances, Wilbur," O'Shea said. "Mr. Gilliam is set to give you one more, but you've got to take it right now!"

"What the hell is the meaning of this?"

The voice came along with a set of heavy footsteps scrambling against the dirt. A squat, tubby figure separated from the shadows, but it was the huge hat on top of Sheriff Donner's head that truly gave him away. The lawman had one deputy with him and they both stopped so they could keep all four of Gilliam's boys in their sights.

"This don't concern you, Sheriff," O'Shea said.

"The hell it doesn't! What do you intend to do with them torches?"

"You can go ask Mr. Gilliam. He'll be plenty happy to—"

"I'm asking you, O'Shea," Donner interrupted. "So I suggest that you start talking to me right here and now before I drag all four of you into my jail."

O'Shea put his back to the door and took a few steps toward the lawman. He stopped once he was within ten yards of Donner. "This house belongs to Mr. Gilliam."

Sheriff Donner looked over to his deputy before returning O'Shea's glare. "What the hell are you talking about now?"

"Wilbur Johanssen owes Mr. Gilliam enough for his property to start getting seized."

"Do you even know what that means?"

"Yeah. This house belongs to Mr. Gilliam. Go see him and he'll show you the paperwork."

"I'll do that. Until then, I'm going to have to ask you to step away from that house and put them torches out."

"This is Mr. Gilliam's property and he wants to burn it

down. This is a free country, so he can do whatever he wants with his property."

Donner squared his shoulders and put a steely edge into his voice. "Ain't nobody starting a fire in this town. I don't give a damn who owns what, I won't have anyone putting us all at risk. You light that house and the fire could spread throughout this whole damn place."

A few moments passed where nobody said a word. All that could be heard was the rustle of the wind and the crackle of the flames sputtering atop the torches.

Finally, O'Shea looked to the men surrounding him and said, "You two men, get going. We don't want any trouble."

Before either of the other men could question the order, they saw the subtle nod of O'Shea's head which was followed by a wink. The nod pointed them toward the backside of the house and the wink wasn't too difficult to interpret from there.

"Okay," one of the men said. "Sure."

With that, the two men lowered their torches and started walking around the house. As soon as they were able to break away from the main group, they hastened their steps until they were able to jog around to the back of the house. They could still hear the voices belonging to the sheriff and O'Shea, but they ignored them for the most part.

"Should we start burning the place?" one of the two men asked once they were both around the house.

The second one nodded. "I'd say so. O'Shea said this would happen and if it did, we should just torch the place and worry about whatever comes after that."

"All right then. Let's do this and get out of here."

Suddenly, the sound of something scraping against the dirt could just barely be heard. That sound was soon followed by a low, whispering voice.

"I don't think so," the voice said.

Both men turned around to look while he extended his

arm to brush the torch along Wilbur's house. In one instant, the torch was snatched from his hand. In the next, a fist was speeding from out of nowhere to knock his head damn near off his shoulders.

The second man with the torch barely got a chance to get a look at Clint's face before all of this had happened. Although he managed to get his wits about him in less than a second or two, that was still too late to avoid what was coming next.

Clint took a lunging step forward from where he'd been hiding with his back against a wall. Using the momentum of that step along with the force of his own muscles, he nearly broke his knuckles against the gunman's face.

The end was quick and painless. When the gunman fell, it was as though his upper body was tied to a load of rocks. He let the torch slide from his hand as he slumped straight back to catch up on his sleep.

Clint's free hand acted on instinct, and in plenty of time to catch the second torch before it hit the ground. "Stay where you are, Wilbur," Clint said to the man still waiting in the shadows. "I'll take care of this myself."

After what he'd just seen, Wilbur wasn't about to talk back.

THIRTY-NINE

"Where'd you send those two?" Donner asked.

O'Shea had the torch in hand, but his arms lowered to swing at his sides. "I sent them away. Isn't that what you wanted?"

"I also wanted you to snuff them torches." Turning to his deputy, the sheriff said, "Go check on them other two."

The remaining gunman next to O'Shea stepped forward and dropped his hand dangerously close to the gun at his side. "Let 'em be," he snarled.

O'Shea started to try and call the other man off, but the deputy had already stepped in to speak for himself.

"Don't you move toward that gun," the deputy warned.

Now, Donner was also trying to take control of the situation, but things had already gone too far for that. Before the sheriff could get a word out or make one more gesture, the gunman next to O'Shea had already shifted his hand one too many times.

The deputy could tell that he was going to be staring down the wrong end of a pistol if he didn't act fast. His hand moved for his holster, but it had also been trembling. That tremble snagged his thumb against his holster for a fraction of a second, but that was more than enough to give the other man the advantage.

The gunman next to O'Shea smirked even as his hand was bringing up his pistol. He could tell already that he was going to outdraw the lawman in front of him. As soon as his hand came to a stop, his finger tightened around the trigger, sending a tongue of smoke and flame from his weapon.

That single gunshot blasted through the air. Since everyone else in the area wasn't making a peep, the sound of lead punching through flesh and bone could be heard by everyone there.

The deputy stood his ground for a moment, blinking one eye rapidly while still fumbling for his gun. His other eye wasn't blinking because it was no longer there. The other man's bullet had entered just beneath the deputy's eye socket and exited out the top of his skull.

A crimson mist rained down behind the deputy. Judging by the look on his face, the younger lawman might have even felt the mist before he finally dropped over into a lifeless heap.

Sheriff Donner had been stricken dumb by the lightning-quick turn of events. He wasn't alone in that regard since O'Shea was also still in the same position he'd been in before the shot had gone off. Now, both men came to their senses and reacted to what they'd just seen.

"Son of a bitch," Donner grunted as his own hand slapped against the gun holstered at his side.

O'Shea cursed to himself as he saw everything spiral out of control. He knew this fight would come sooner or later, but it wasn't supposed to happen just yet. That thought flashed through his mind as he prepared to clear leather and drop the old fart that had been a thorn in Gilliam's side for a bit too long.

There was no question in O'Shea's mind that he could take the lawman. Even as his hand wrapped around the grip of his pistol, he knew that he was miles ahead of the sheriff. That was why he was so surprised when O'Shea heard the crack of gunfire as something ripped through his rib cage.

The wound was shallow, but it was enough to break has stride as well as his concentration. It was also enough to allow Donner to draw and take a shot of his own. Unfortunately, that shot hissed well over O'Shea's head.

Just as the lawman was squeezing the trigger, the gunman beside O'Shea was able to shift his aim and send another piece of lead in his direction. With the roar of the pistol still echoing in his ears, the gunman had no chance of hearing the footsteps that were rushing up behind him.

Something knocked against the back of his skull and soon he was looking up at the stars. The world seemed to tilt beneath him, but the gunman was the one doing the tilting. In fact, he was tilting back to the ground and lying stretched out in the dirt a moment later. Once he'd dropped, Wilbur was shown to be standing right behind him. The rock he'd used to knock the gunman out was still in his hand.

That only left O'Shea and Donner standing looking at each other. Both of them were confused as hell and still glancing at the wound that seemed to have appeared in O'Shea's ribs.

Although he was fairly certain he wasn't the one to put that wound there, Sheriff Donner was just thankful that the gunman beside O'Shea had missed the last shot he'd taken before getting knocked out.

"Drop the gun, O'Shea!" Donner hollered.

O'Shea touched a hand against the wound in his side and turned to look behind him. He could see a shadowy figure approaching him, but knew that he wouldn't be able to turn and fire before that figure put him down. Focusing on the sheriff, O'Shea also realized that he wouldn't be able to raise his gun and fire at full speed. His wound sent stabbing pain through his whole torso just at the thought of moving like that.

Donner stepped closer, keeping his gun trained on O'Shea even as his hand started to tremble. "You'd best drop that gun. I'm warning you!"

"Or you'll do what?" O'Shea snarled. "You ain't nothing more than half a lawman anyway. You couldn't even hit the broad side of a barn."

"Best for you not to test that."

"Yeah?" O'Shea said after thinking it over for a second.

In the next second, O'Shea gritted his teeth and lifted his gun to point it at the sheriff. Donner's eyes widened in genuine surprise at the move, but his finger was already tightening around the trigger out of pure reflex.

That reflex saved the lawman's life by sending a round into O'Shea's chest and dropping him into the dirt. Even as the gunman spat his dying breath into the dirt, Donner stood over him with disbelief in his eyes. His hand twitched upward when he spotted a figure step out of the shadows from a spot behind O'Shea.

"Easy, Sheriff," Clint said as he holstered his Colt and raised both hands. "I'd say things are well in hand here."

The lawman was reluctant to lower his weapon. In fact, his eyes twitched toward any sound that came from any direction. "That you, Adams?"

"It sure is. I took care of them two that went around back with torches. Wilbur will help you drag them into a cell so they can wake up behind bars."

"So you were the one who . . ." Although the question trailed off, Donner's eyes were focusing in on O'Shea's body.

"I clipped him a little," Clint said. "Just to even the odds. I figured you could handle it from there."

Although plenty of men would have taken offense to Clint's assumption that the odds were in favor of O'Shea to begin with, Donner wasn't one of them. He nodded slowly and finally dropped his gun into its holster. "Guess I'm not as good a shot as I thought."

Already, Clint could see a difference in Sheriff Donner's face. There was a humility in his eyes that hadn't been there before. There was also a bit more wisdom in there as well.

"You did just fine, Sheriff," Clint said. "He didn't give you much choice."

"At least this is over."

"Well, not just yet. There's a bit more to wrap up and I'm going to need a little more help from you to do it."

Donner nodded. "You got it."

Looking around to the people who'd gathered to watch the fight, Clint said, "I'm also going to need something from you folks."

FORTY

Gilliam hadn't been able to sit still since he'd last seen O'Shea. During that entire time, he'd been pacing back and forth in front of his office window while trying to take a fresh look out every time he passed it. His palms were sweating by now and his fingers were clenching tightly together.

"I should be seeing flames by now," Gilliam seethed. "Or I should be able to smell smoke. Maybe hear people shouting."

Mace stood close by. His face was as passive as always. His arms were folded neatly across his chest.

"You think that sheriff got to them?"

Mace shook his head slowly. "I doubt the sheriff's moved that fast in his whole life. Even if he did get there, he wouldn't be able to stop O'Shea."

"That's true," Gilliam said, nodding quickly. "Maybe the fire's just getting started."

As if to answer his questions, Gilliam heard some commotion coming from one of the floors below him in the gentlemen's club. His eyes grew wide and he spun around to look at Mace.

"Go see what that's all about," Gilliam ordered.

Nodding once, Mace stepped from the room and headed down to the second floor.

After just a few minutes had passed, Mace returned.

"You might want to come down here, Mr. Gilliam."

Thankful for a reason to leave his office, Gilliam rushed past Mace and stomped down the stairs. He kept going until he was in the lounge on the first floor. Once there, he stopped and turned toward Mace who was following directly behind him.

"And what am I supposed to be looking at?" Gilliam asked.

Mace stood at the bottom of the stairs. From there, he turned toward the main sitting area and pointed a finger to a man making himself comfortable on a padded chaise lounge.

"Evening, Mr. Gilliam," Clint said with a tip of his hat.

Gilliam stepped forward and placed his hands upon his hips. A smile worked its way onto his face that made him look like a hungry wolf. "There you are. Did you bring your friend, the gambler, with you?"

"Wilbur? No. I came to have a word with you myself."

"Speaking on his behalf, huh? I heard plenty about you, but I never expected The Gunsmith to be representing petty losers like Wilbur Johanssen."

"This has to do with some other business that concerned me more directly," Clint said. "Namely, the men you sent to kill me at my hotel."

Gilliam's eyes narrowed and he took a slow look around the room. Although there were plenty of people there, they were more interested in working their way out of the room than listening in. Besides, all he could see were regular customers and working girls.

"Why would I want to send anyone to kill you?" Gilliam asked.

"Maybe because I spoke up for someone you intended on milking until they either went broke or died. Or it could also have been that I stumbled upon one of your girls who decided they weren't afraid of you anymore and didn't like being held captive."

When he said that, Clint noticed that some of the girls around him seemed confused. Others lowered their eyes and started to fidget in a very worried manner.

Gilliam had been looking at the girls as well and he saw the same things. After he'd caused all the worried girls to avert their eyes, he shifted his gaze back to Clint. "You can't prove a damn bit of that and if you keep defaming my name that way, I'll have charges brought against you."

"Really?" Clint stood up and made his way over to a fireplace. Leaning against it, he asked, "Where's Jack?"

"Jack's a fiery young man. He's either drunk somewhere or might have gotten himself into a bit of trouble that wouldn't have a damn thing to do with me."

"All right then. And what about Estrella? Does she have anything to do with you?"

Suddenly, Gilliam began to get just as uncomfortable as some of the women in the room. He put on a smile, but the edge beneath it was plain enough to see.

"You want to talk business?" Gilliam asked. "You want to discuss personal matters? I say we do it without an audience. Otherwise, you can take your ass out of my club."

"Fine. How about the Second Chance Saloon?"

Gilliam grinned like a shark in bloody water. "Perfect."

FORTY-ONE

When Clint got there, the Second Chance Saloon was practically empty. Any notion that this was a coincidence lasted right up until he saw Mace personally ushering out a drunk local. The gunman shoved the staggering man down the street and then nodded toward Clint.

"Mr. Gilliam will be right here."

Clint gave a nod in return and stepped inside.

It seemed fitting for the night to end up in this spot. He'd met Wilbur Johanssen just outside those doors. In fact, bits of dirt in the street were still spattered with some of Wilbur's blood. But this wasn't going to be about the blood Wilbur or anyone else had spilled.

It was going to be about second chances and hard luck.

Some people deserved the former and others deserved the latter. Whichever one was coming, Clint was going to see that it got delivered to the proper people.

When Clint stepped inside, he noticed that Mace hadn't had enough time to clear out the place entirely. There were still a few tables occupied as well as a few card games taking place at tables scattered throughout the saloon. The bar had a few occupants, but there wasn't enough going on to keep Clint's steps from echoing as he picked a table next to a small stage and sat down.

Before too long, the door swung open again. The doorway was filled by Gilliam's bulky frame as he stuffed his hands into a pair of leather gloves and looked around for where Clint was sitting. Before the door could close, however, there was a slight commotion coming from outside.

Accompanied by a set of frantic footsteps, the words echoed down the street as the person shouting them ran right past the saloon. ". . . ned down! The Johanssen place burned down! The Johanssen pl . . ."

When he turned back around, Gilliam was grinning from ear to ear. He couldn't have looked more pleased with himself as he walked over to Clint's table, pulled out a chair and dropped himself into it.

"Hell of a night," Gilliam rasped.

Clint allowed a glimmer of regret to pass over his face. "Yeah," he said sadly. "It sure is."

Gilliam ate that up like it was candy. "I wouldn't worry too much about your friend. He was on his way down way before you showed up."

"Sure he was. And that suited you just fine, didn't it?"

Gilliam shrugged. He was so content with the cards he was holding at the moment that he barely seemed to bother putting on his poker face. "I'm not the only one cashing in on interest payments."

"Is that what you call it? I thought it seemed more like you were bleeding people dry."

"Nobody forced him to borrow my money."

"Just like nobody kept track of whatever money he repaid."

Gilliam raised his hand and snapped his fingers until a server came over to take their drink orders. Once the

woman was gone, he folded both hands neatly upon the
table. "As much as I'd like to sit around and talk about poor
Wilbur, it won't get us anywhere. As far as I'm concerned,
his debt is almost paid."

"Taking his house wasn't enough?"

Gilliam shook his head slowly. The smile on his lips
didn't even start to fade. "That took care of his interest and
it set a damn fine example in the process." Leaning forward, he stared at Clint with eyes that grew wide and
somewhat wild. "Businesses will fall in line with my way
of thinking and that goes right down to the owners of this
town."

Allowing himself to let an interested look slip onto his
face, Clint leaned forward a bit as well. "You mean Mark
Bradshaw?"

Picking up on Clint's interest instantly, Gilliam nodded. "He's been chasing his tail since he staked his claim
here. I've tried to buy in, but he never saw the benefits I
offered. Now, I won't need him. I'll take this place for myself and maybe throw him a bone. That is, if I'm feeling
generous."

"And why tell me all this?" Clint asked.

"Because I'm giving you an opportunity."

The server returned with the drinks and Gilliam remained quiet until she left. Before he started talking again,
he shot a look toward the front door just to make sure that
Mace was still there.

"I'm giving you an opportunity because you won it."
Glancing around, Gilliam opened his arms as if to embrace the entire saloon. "You're getting a second
chance, which makes this place a great choice for this
little chat." After taking a sip of the whiskey he'd ordered, Gilliam added, "You backed the wrong horse,
Adams. But that doesn't mean I'm not willing to let you
make up for it."

"And after all that's happened, why would I even consider this?" Clint asked.

"Because, if you play your cards wrong here, I'll see to it that you don't leave this room alive."

FORTY-TWO

Clint knew a bluff when he heard one.

After playing cards in anything but a friendly game, that skill was vital for survival. Some bluffs snuck in like a snake on its belly, but there was something else that stuck out even more than a bad lie. It was something that was also critical for any gambler to recognize.

The truth.

When Gilliam spoke, he did so as if he wasn't even making a threat. He spoke with such utter confidence and certainty that he was either totally convinced that his claim was true or he was one of the best actors in the world. Since Gilliam was sitting next to the saloon's stage and not on it, Clint was more inclined to pick the former rather than the latter.

Clint took a moment to let the words sink in. Not only did that make Gilliam even more smug in his position, but it allowed Clint to take another look around the saloon. There were still a few people here and there, but they seemed to be wrapped up in business of their own. Mace could be seen standing at the front door, but his back was turned and hadn't moved from that spot.

Then again, Clint had seen oak trees move more on a windy day than Mace had the entire time he'd been in town.

"Who's going to follow through on that promise?" Clint asked. "You?"

Gilliam scooted out from the table just enough for Clint to see the gun holstered at his side. "I didn't get where I am by making empty threats. I got where I am by making sure I got the right cards and then playing them right. Men like Wilbur Johanssen have made me rich. Even if they do get on a winning streak, a little creative dealing is all I need to see things swing my way again."

Now that had taken Clint a little by surprise. "You cheated?" he asked.

"Only once," Gilliam said. "And it was just to push Wilbur over the edge. Once that happened, he was right where I needed him to be for him to come running to me. It's like fishing, really. Every so often, you need to tug the line a bit to make sure the hook gets sunk in nice and deep."

"Is that how you got Estrella to sign on to work for you?"

Although Gilliam twitched a bit at that, it wasn't anything that another sip of whiskey couldn't fix. "She's a beauty, all right. Then again, I figure you've seen that for yourself. Tell me something, Adams. When she asked for you to get her away from me, did she promise to fuck you? If so, then you're one up on me. That bitch's legs have been closed so tight that I was starting to think they'd been sewn together."

Rather than show what he was truly thinking just then, Clint smiled slightly and nodded.

Tugging the line.

Sinking in the hook.

"She said something about a few other girls you keep at that club," Clint said. "She made it sound like a private harem."

Gilliam smiled and raised his glass. "I like the sound of that. You wouldn't believe how much men will pay for the company of a lady. Most men like to rent a few minutes or maybe an hour. But there are some who want more than that. They like to own rather than rent." Winking, he added, "That's where the real money is."

So far, Clint hadn't touched the beer that had been brought for him. Now, he picked it up. Looking down into the foamy brew, he said, "You're right. I never knew about any of that. Of course, I'm not a pimp and I don't need to pay for my women, so there's no reason I should know about it."

The smile remained on Gilliam's face for a moment, but it seemed to rot from the inside out as all the levity behind it was sucked dry. Soon, that smile looked more like it was plastered on the face of a skull before it dropped off completely.

"I don't pay any of those girls," Gilliam hissed. He slammed his glass against the table and once that fell from his grasp, he pounded his fist against it instead, "They're mine. They agreed to that, and I make them earn their keep. They do what I say because I'm the one who took them from whatever shithole they left behind and bought them clothes, paid for their food and gave them a good place to live. They don't earn their keep and they pay the price for it."

"What do you do? Slap them around?"

Gilliam stood up quick enough to send his chair clattering on the floor behind him. Leaning forward like a vulture, he rasped, "You got two choices right now. Accept the generous offer I'm handing you or you can wind up in a hole next to those whores and gamblers you're so fond of.

"In fact, I've got a fresh little Chinese girl to keep you company. We haven't even covered her up yet. And before much longer, Mark Bradshaw will be right in there as well."

Even the best poker players had their limits. Clint could look at any hand with the same amount of apathy, but he wasn't able to keep his face straight when he heard that. Of course, he didn't really want to let that go unnoticed.

"You know I'm telling the truth," Gilliam said with a nod. "Just like you know I can kill you if you don't say just what I want to hear. You got nowhere to run, Adams. Your friend Bradshaw is too stupid to know who's really running this town and the law around here is too lazy to do anything but grow a fat ass and collect bullshit taxes. He's nothing to me and neither are you."

"That's not a very nice thing to say. Is it, Mark?"

Gilliam looked stunned at first and then confused.

Clint, on the other hand, was wearing the smile that Gilliam had left behind.

"It sure isn't," came a voice from the back of the saloon.

Gilliam shifted around just in time to see Mark Bradshaw walk in from the saloon's rear entrance.

"What's going on here?" Gilliam asked.

"Seems to me that you're digging your own grave," Clint said.

FORTY-THREE

"You're through here, Gilliam," Clint said. "Now that the man you were going to bury knows what you're up to, you might as well forget those plans to take over this town."

Rage flashed in Gilliam's eyes.

"And you can forget about your other business as well," another voice said from over Clint's shoulder.

The newest voice may have been feminine, but it was more fiery than Clint's and Bradshaw's combined. Stepping out from one of the narrow doors leading behind the stage, Kathy stomped forward and walked straight up to Gilliam. She ignored the man's gun completely as she reached out and slapped Gilliam across the face.

"That's for what you did to those poor girls," she said. "I feel sick for not knowing about what you've done, but since I can't slap myself . . ." She finished that statement by slapping the other side of Gilliam's face so that both cheeks turned beet red under the impact.

Gilliam snarled like an animal and balled both hands into fists. Before he could rear back a punch, his target was pulled out of his reach. Estrella leaned out from the same stage door that Kathy had used and pulled the other woman back.

"Glad to see everyone got here on time," Clint said as he stepped in to make sure Gilliam didn't make another move toward the ladies.

Gilliam was letting out his breath in short bursts. After he saw Kathy was out of his reach, he turned to look at Bradshaw. The Texan wasn't alone, either. He was standing protectively in front of Daisy Johanssen.

"Thanks for bringing everyone to the party, ladies," Clint said with a tip of his hat. "You were right on time."

With that, both women pulled their escorts back. They calmed them down and kept them from doing anything else by telling them exactly what Clint had told them to say before they'd gotten to town.

Stepping back as though he'd had five glasses of whiskey instead of just one, Gilliam put some space between himself and Clint. "This doesn't change anything, Adams," he said in a scratchy rasp. "Not between you and me."

"You've got no cards left to play, Gilliam," Clint said. "You don't even scare anyone any longer. After tonight, everyone will see you for what you are. And whatever killers you want to hire will find out that you couldn't even crack down on a simple man who overplayed a few hands of cards. Wilbur's fine. His house is all in order, and that's a hell of a lot more than I can say about you."

"What? How do you know this?" Gilliam asked.

"Because I was there. I meant to have Wilbur here with me as well to help you spout off some more to incriminate yourself, but he's busy dragging the men you sent into jail or to the undertaker. Besides, it turns out that you did just fine spouting off without much help from anyone else."

When Gilliam looked around at the faces surrounding him, he knew Clint was telling the truth. Kathy was fuming and trying to get her hands on him so that meant that his business at Rosie's was finished. Mark Bradshaw might not have been so animated, but the look in his eyes spoke volumes. When a man like Bradshaw looked at you like that, it meant your business in that entire state was finished.

The wild look in Gilliam's eyes became even wilder until he sucked in a deep breath and squared off with Clint. "I still have one more card to play, Adams. If I'm going down, I'll see to it that I take a few of you sons of bitches with me."

Clint stepped back from the table and put on a cool, steely-eyed expression. "You've played this through like a snake this far. At least put it to rest like a man. At least you have a chance going up against a judge. You won't have a fraction of that chance against me."

"Oh, I think I've got a better chance than you think. I'm not the only one to make preparations for this meeting."

"All right then. Have it your way."

His eyes widening as he nodded slowly, Gilliam said, "Oh, I intend on doing that very thing."

Clint kept his eyes open and searching. He didn't have to wait long before Gilliam made his move.

Gilliam snapped his arm out and dropped it straight down.

Clint responded immediately to it by snatching the Colt from its holster and firing off four shots in two quick bursts. One pair of rounds flew off to Gilliam's right and the other two hissed through the air to Gilliam's left.

At first, Gilliam looked like he was about to do a happy jig. Then, he began looking around with an unspoken question written all over his face.

"What's the matter, Gilliam?" Clint asked. "Still waiting to hear from those aces you planted up your sleeve?"

As if on cue, two men took a few staggering steps and made a gurgling, pained grunting noise. One of the men had been at the bar and the other had been at one of the card tables. Both of them had guns in their hands and were cut short before they could respond to Gilliam's signal to fire.

"I spotted those men you planted as soon as I got here," Clint said while lowering his Colt. "Too bad for you I'm so good at remembering faces."

"Go to hell, Adams!" Gilliam shouted as he reached for the gun at his side.

Gilliam's draw was quick. It wasn't quick enough, however, to get a shot off before Clint lifted his gun and squeezed his trigger.

The bullet caught Gilliam through the heart, exploding it within his chest. The silver-haired man dropped to his knees as his gun slid out through his fingers to thump onto the floor.

"Go to . . . hell," were his last words.

Shaking his head, Clint replied, "Not today." Looking up, he saw Mace standing just inside the saloon's front door. "The sheriff will be coming by shortly. You can take your chances with him or me."

Mace didn't say a word. Instead, his eyes flickered from one dead body to another before coming to rest upon the Colt in Clint's hand. The gun's smoking barrel was still pointed at Gilliam. Mace's own gun was less than two inches from his hand.

"All those shots kind of blend together, don't they?" Clint asked. "Hard to keep track of them all."

Mace glanced back to the fallen gunmen. The one at the card table had a hole in his chest and one through his shoulder. The one on the floor by the bar had a face full of blood, but the mirror on the wall behind him was cracked in two separate places. Although he couldn't see Gilliam so well, he figured he knew enough to put things straight in his own mind.

Clint let Mace sift through his thoughts and try to count up how many shots had been fired. He knew he wouldn't be able to talk any sense into the gunman. Whatever was about to happen, it was going to be Mace's call.

Mace made that call in a fraction of a second, deciding his own fate in the process.

Mace's hand dropped to his gun and drew it in less time than it took a man to blink. Clint's hand moved as well to shift the Colt's aim and pull his trigger.

Both guns went off at the same time. Both bullets whipped past each other in the smoky air.

One bullet grazed through a few layers of skin before burying itself into a wall. The other drilled through flesh and bone before finding a similar resting spot.

Clint reached up to feel the bloody scrape that had been torn in his cheek.

Mace stood upon wobbly legs, blinking as blood from the fresh hole in his forehead dripped blood down into his eye. "You only . . . had . . . one bullet."

"Yeah," Clint said. "And it had your name on it."

FORTY-FOUR

Clint held up a thin glass made out of expensive crystal. The glass was quickly met by an identical twin that was clinked gently against it.

"I don't normally get the chance to drink much champagne," he said.

Sitting across from him, Estrella smiled and took a sip from her own glass. "Well, after the way things turned out, I'd say you earned it. Wilbur and his wife got their house. Their debt is repaid and they're back to their normal life.

"Kathy's running a straight-shooting cathouse with no complaints from the customers or any of her girls. Even Sheriff Donner got the lead out of his ass and started acting like a real sheriff instead of some tax collector. I'll bet you never bargained for all of this to come about."

Clint sipped the champagne, winced and set down the glass. "Not hardly. I was expecting to take a job for Bradshaw getting his saloons off the ground."

"Is that so?"

"Yep. All I did to that end was tell him to make the places the kinds of saloons a professional gambler would want to see. After that, they'll flock to them in droves."

"Is that what you were telling him that night after all the smoke cleared?"

"Nope," Clint said. "I told him that once the word spread about how Gilliam was dealt with and the law was being enforced by a man too rich to bribe, Los Tejanos would be on the gambler's circuit in no time."

"Really?" Estrella asked with a wary tilt of her head.

Clint nodded. "Cheaters are the only ones who love to play at crooked tables in crooked towns. The big money comes from real gamblers. They prefer to play their cards rather than worry about ending up with a bullet in their back."

"I guess that makes sense." After draining the last of her champagne, Estrella set her glass down and walked around the table. Standing in front of Clint, she straddled his lap and lowered herself down onto him. "Now that I've got a place of my own, I'll have to keep that in mind."

Clint's hands moved over her hips and then around her waist. "Speaking of which, this is a hell of a nice place you bought."

"An old friend of mine needed a partner and I just happened to get enough money from Gilliam before he cashed out."

Clint gave her a vaguely surprised look. "I thought you didn't do much for him apart from serve drinks and talk to customers."

"Let's just say that I was sneaking around that office of his way before you rode into town, Clint Adams."

"You're nothing but a thief," he said as he took hold of Estrella and picked her up as he got to his feet.

Estrella let out a surprised squeal, but hung on for the

ride as Clint carried her over to the large bed which took up most of their suite.

After laying her down on the mattress, Clint moved his hands up and down her body, slowly tugging her clothes open and then peeling them off her body. "How'd you like it if someone came along to take something from you?" he asked, taking away her blouse and then moving on to her skirt.

"I couldn't stand the thought of it," Estrella replied, even as she lifted her bottom off the bed to allow her skirt to be removed completely. "In fact," she added as Clint removed the thin white slip she'd been wearing, "it would be an absolute crime."

Clint looked down at her naked body as he began to remove his own clothes. "Then I guess that'd make me guilty."

After that, he crawled onto the bed and on top of Estrella's waiting form. Her nipples became erect as he got closer. When he finally lowered himself down, she let out a contented sigh.

Opening her legs for him, Estrella closed her eyes and savored the feel of Clint entering her. She propped one foot on the edge of the bed so she could pump her hips up and down as he slid his cock inside of her.

When he was fully in her, Clint slid his hands along her arms until they were stretched out over her head on the mattress. From there, he clasped her hands as he pumped into her one time and then slid his hands back down along her smooth skin one more time.

She was writhing beneath him now, smiling and moaning softly under her breath. The sheets beneath her were made of satin and a few candles flickered from tables on either side of the bed. The soft light played across her skin to make it seem almost creamy in texture.

Clint's hands kept moving along her sides; his fingers brushing against the plump curve of her breasts. He heard her pull in an expectant breath as his thumbs drew close to her nipples, but Clint made her wait just a bit longer.

He could feel the tension translate all the way through her body. Her abdomen grew more solid beneath him and the muscles in her legs tightened as well. Even the lips between her legs closed around his cock as if to massage him as he moved in and out of her in a slow, insistent rhythm.

Finally, he took hold of her breasts and squeezed them in his hands. Estrella let out a moan, which only grew louder as Clint pumped even harder between her legs.

She opened her eyes and smiled hungrily at him while taking hold of his hips to guide every other thrust. After entwining one leg around him, she arched her back and slipped one hand down over her stomach to linger at the spot where their bodies connected.

As Clint bucked on top of her, their bodies slid slowly up the satin sheets and along the surface of the bed. They were rocking against the headboard by the time Estrella wriggled out from beneath him. She settled on top of Clint and lowered herself onto him, taking in every inch of his penis until she was ready to grab hold of the bed and start riding him in earnest.

Their groans filled the room for the rest of the night as well as a good part of the night after that. Outside their room, more and more people were taking notice of the newest place to reopen after coming under new management. The card tables were full, the gambling was honest and the liquor was flowing like water.

By all accounts, not a bad start for the Third Chance Saloon.

Watch for

THE LAST RIDE

282nd novel in the exciting GUNSMITH
series from Jove

Coming in June!

J. R. ROBERTS

THE GUNSMITH

GIANT ACTION! GIANT ADVENTURE!

THE GUNSMITH

GIANT

GIANT WESTERNS FEATURING THE GUNSMITH

THE GHOST OF BILLY THE KID
0-515-13622-0

LITTLE SURESHOT AND THE
WILD WEST SHOW
0-515-13851-7

**AVAILABLE WHEREVER BOOKS ARE SOLD OR AT
WWW.PENGUIN.COM**

J799

JAKE LOGAN
TODAY'S HOTTEST ACTION WESTERN!

9

FROM **TOM CALHOUN**

THE TEXAS BOUNTY HUNTER SERIES
FEATURING RELENTLESS MANHUNTER
J.T. LAW

**TEXAS TRACKER:
JUSTICE IN BIG SPRINGS**
0-515-13850-9

**TEXAS TRACKER:
SHADOW IN AUSTIN**
0-515-13898-3